The Dark Ride

Ride

Kill Minus 9 - Book 1

J. Andrew O'Donnell

J. Andrew O'Donnell

This is a work of fiction. Any references to historical events, real people, real places, or real products are used fictiously. Names, characters, and places are products of the author's imagination.

Contents

Acknowledgements

Kill Minus 9 – Book 1
The Dark Ride

Written by J. Andrew O'Donnell
Edited by Skylar Burris
Cover design by Amy Kenny
Illustrations by David "Shalock" Neito
Beta Readers:
Virginia O'Donnell & Carrie Newman

A note to the reader:

The following book contains episodes 1-57 of my serialized novel Kill Minus 9.

This series was originally published on a one-episode-per-week basis on the Amazon Kindle Vella platform.

Each of the Kindle Vella episodes contained "Author's Notes" sections at the end of each chapter. In order to maintain a more continuous flow for the book version, I've elected to remove the "Author's Notes" that followed each chapter, and I have instead placed them collectively in the "Author's Notes" section at the end of this book.

If you enjoy this book and want to catch up on the latest episodes (episode 58 and beyond), check out Kill Minus 9 on Amazon Kindle Vella for the newest chapters. The remaining future episodes will be compiled into Book 2.

I hope you enjoy reading this as much as I've enjoyed writing it.

-J. Andrew O'Donnell

1

DARKNESS

A dam opened his eyes. He could see only darkness above him. It seemed as if he were outdoors, but there were no stars in the sky or clouds visible. He was lying flat on his back on what felt like concrete. No bed, no pillow, just hard, flat ground and darkness. What had happened? Where was he? Why was he there? He couldn't remember anything except his name: Adam Justice. He knew that much for certain, but he couldn't recall much else. He tried to remember how he got to wherever he currently was but couldn't recall anything at all. Adam sat up and looked around.

The ground was not concrete as he had first thought. Adam ran his hand over it. It was almost like a black glass surface, smooth to the touch and seemingly reflective. He looked around and found darkness everywhere. The only thing illuminating anything was a distant blue glow somewhere far beyond his current location. The flat glass ground seemed to go on forever. The soft blue glow in the distance looked as if a cyan blue sun had dipped down past the horizon.

Adam gazed off into the distance. There were no trees, no buildings, no hills or mountains. Just flatness and that eerie blue light in the distance. Adam began to look himself over. He was wearing what felt and looked like medical scrubs. There wasn't enough light to tell what color they were. He thought they might be hospital green, but he couldn't know for sure. Was he a doctor? He couldn't remember. Why couldn't he remember? What is this place? Why am I here? he thought to himself.

There were no sounds at all, nothing to help him figure out his situation. No birds, no crickets, no rustling leaves. He could only hear the sound of his own breathing and the faint thud of his heartbeat.

"HELLO?" he shouted. His voice did not echo off of anything in the distance.

"IS THERE ANYONE OUT THERE?" No response. Nothing. Adam began walking in no particular direction. He was merely moving away from where he was. There was nothing to walk toward as an end goal. The landscape (or lack thereof) was the same in every direction. Flatness for miles.

"What the hell is this place?" Adam muttered to himself. He stopped walking and took a break to gather his thoughts. He was not hungry, nor thirsty, nor tired. Maybe I'm in a dream. Maybe I'm in a coma. Maybe this is all some sort of hallucination.

Adam resumed walking and realized at that moment that he was barefoot. He could feel the coldness of the glass-like floor underneath his feet. He kept walking for what seemed like an eternity. Minutes became hours, or so it seemed. He really had no concept of time. The blue glow had looked like a setting sun, but its position remained fixed on the horizon. Am I in hell? What if hell isn't fire and brimstone? What if hell is just a big empty endless expanse of nothingness where you wander aimlessly without anything to occupy your mind? Fear began to creep into Adam's thoughts. What if I go insane from all this nothingness?

Adam figured he had walked at least a mile or so by now. He didn't know whether he was walking in circles or in one direction, as there were no fixed objects with which to orient himself. Adam was growing more and more hopeless with each passing step. Is this it? Is this all there is? Suddenly, out of nowhere, he heard a low rumbling sound almost like thunder. Adam saw a faint bluish gray cloud appear about one hundred meters in front of him. It was at ground level, as if a ground fog had emerged and formed a small cloud that obscured something behind it. Lightning bolts formed within the cloud and caused it to brighten as if it were a small storm cloud. He ran toward it unafraid, happy to see something new instead of the unending blank space he had been staring into for hours.

2
SOMETHING
RED

W hat could it be? Adam continued running toward the mysterious ground fog. It was dissipating now, and he could see something behind it. Something red. The suspense was killing him. What the hell is it? He looked it over. As strange as it seemed, the object was exactly what he thought it was: a red motorcycle. It looked almost identical to a 1997 Ducati 1098S, but it was missing the Ducati badging. Why do I know this information? he wondered briefly before straddling the bike. This wasn't just any motorcycle. It was a high-performance sports bike, sometimes called a "superbike." It would have cost close to $20,000 when it was brand new, way more than an average motorcycle at the time.

Even in the dark blackness around him, Adam could see the beautiful, candy apple red, flawless finish of the bike. Not a scratch on it, as if it had just left the showroom floor. The foot pegs felt harsh against his bare feet, but he didn't care right now. He instinctively pressed the ignition switch and started the engine as if he had done it a hundred times before, not even needing to fumble around to find the starter. The engine purred to life. It was so nice to hear something other than the sound of his own breathing. The engine drone was soothing and comforting in the vast empty void. It was something different, and that was exactly what he needed right now after he had been on the verge of losing his sanity from the lack of sensory input.

He revved the engine slightly. Before he knew it, he was off, wearing no helmet, and gliding forward in the darkness on his red steed. Something about how the bike moved was off, though. He couldn't quite figure out what was wrong, but he really didn't care right now. His headlight carved into darkness ahead of him, revealing nothing but the glassy floor and the blue light on the horizon.

Adam drove and drove. It felt good to be moving at high speed even though it didn't seem that he was getting closer to any kind of destination. The odometer showed that he had traveled nearly forty miles by now, but he hadn't used hardly any of his gas according to the needle that read FULL. As he rode on, Adam grew worried. If this is a dream, why haven't I woken up yet? What is the purpose of having this motorcycle if I don't have anywhere to go? If it's not a dream, where the hell am I? I can't be in a building. I've been driving for over forty miles. There isn't any building in the world that big. If I'm not in a building, then why are there no stars in the sky? Where is the sun or the moon? What is that strange blue glow in the distance?

He had more questions than answers right now. Still, he kept on riding. Adam told himself he would keep going until he ran out of gas or he found some kind of destination. Something. Anything. There had to be something out there.

A few minutes later, Adam finally spied something in the distance: another lightening-filled cloud, similar to the one the bike had been born out of. This cloud, however, was much larger. So much larger. He drove toward the massive storm cloud on the horizon, throttling up to a breakneck speed. He wanted to get there fast.

As he cruised up to top speed, Adam noticed another curiosity. He felt no movement of air on him. At the speed he was traveling on this sports bike, he should be feeling the wind in his hair. He had ridden bikes like this before without a helmet, and he remembered his eyes getting terribly dry without a visor to keep the wind from drying them out. How on earth is there no wind at the speed I'm going? It was definitely one more odd thing to add to the ever-growing list of odd things he was experiencing in this strange land.

He continued toward the smoky white cloud. Almost there. Wherever "there" happened to be. Adam was ready for something new, or at least he thought he was.

3

OASIS

A dam sped toward the large, glowing, blue-gray storm cloud ahead of him. He had been cruising atop the powerful red motorcycle he had found in the dark abyss earlier. He felt as if he had been riding for at least an hour now. It was hard to tell how long it had really been because the light on the horizon hadn't moved. He could see that the cloud seemed less than a couple of miles from him now. It HAS to be close.

This strange place seemed to go on forever. There were no landmarks to help him get his bearings, save for the cloud he was chasing. Small bolts of lightning illuminated the cloud from within.

Almost there. Just a little bit further. As Adam approached the cloud, it began to dissipate and reveal what was beneath it. The scene was becoming clearer with each second. There was a house. A two-story brick colonial that had been built in the early 1990s by the look of it. The house was strangely familiar, almost too familiar.

I know this house. This looks like my childhood home. Indeed, it did resemble the home where Adam had spent his entire early life until he had left for college. Pieces of memories began to flood back to him as he drove the bike into the empty driveway in front of the house. It was so surreal. The black glass ended at the driveway and then lush green grass began from that point forward. The front yard looked healthy, as if it were springtime.

How is this possible? I must be in some kind of dream or a coma. This house has to be from my memory. That's the only explanation. The house was like an oasis in the desert for Adam. Darkness enveloped everything else around it. It was as if the house had been snatched out of some giant snow globe and plopped down in front of him. There were no neighboring houses or anything else nearby, just his family home. The porch light was on. He could see other lights inside. Adam didn't even venture to try and figure out where the electricity came from that powered the lights in the house. Logic and reason had gone out the window ever since Adam had found himself riding an ethereal red motorcycle in a dark void. He parked the bike in the empty driveway, put down his kickstand, and dismounted. Should I knock? He wondered. He opened the door and walked in.

"Adam, is that you? Dinner is almost ready. How was the drive?"

Adam was taken aback. His mother seemed to appear in the kitchen doorway before him, or at least a 1990s version of his mother, judging by her looks and style of clothing. She gave him a big, warm hug as if she hadn't seen him for quite some time. "How were finals?" she asked. "Do you think you did well? One more semester to go and you'll be a junior. Did you like your professors?"

Adam was hearing words come out of her mouth, but he wasn't really paying attention to them.

"Your dad is out in the garage working on that old car again," she continued. "Sometimes I think he loves it more than me. You better go say hello and tell him to wash up for dinner, ok?"

"Sure thing, mom" was all Adam could muster. What he really wanted to say was "What the hell is this place, and who the hell are you?" but he already knew that this was likely some kind of fever dream. Rather than fight it, he thought he would just lean into it for a bit and play along to see where it went. Adam's memory was starting to come back here and there, and the one thing he knew was that, in current times, his dad had been dead for the last ten years, so even if this wasn't his dad whom he was about to see in the garage, at least it might give him some kind of comfort seeing a ghost, facsimile, or whatever it was out in the garage waiting for him.

Adam walked from the kitchen through the mud room and into the garage. He could see his dad hunched over the open hood of his car, a 1975 Ford Granada. The car was ugly as sin to Adam and everyone else who had ever seen it, but it had character, and his dad loved restoring it.

"Hey, Dad," Adam managed to say as if he had stage fright. His dad looked up and gave him a nod of acknowledgment instead of a warm hug like his mother had. His dad wasn't the most outwardly affectionate person, but Adam knew the man loved him and his mother more than anything in the world.

"Welcome home, son. Glad you had a safe trip. Can you hand me the spark plug gapping tool over on the workbench please?"

Adam handed his dad the tool he had requested. The figure sure looked and sounded like his dad, but something was off. It was the smell. His dad always smelled of chewing tobacco and brake fluid, and there was not a hint of either of those smells anywhere to be found. Adam thought how odd it was that the garage didn't have any smell to it at all. So strange.

"Hey, Dad, can I show you something outside?" Adam asked. He walked over to the garage door opener and pressed the button to open the door.

"Wow! That's a nice bike. Is that a Ducati?" his dad asked as the rollup garage door finished its ascent up the track to the ceiling above them.

"I think so. I'm not sure, but that's not what I wanted you to look at. Do you notice anything wrong out here?" Adam waved his hand around to point at the barren landscape surrounding their island of a house.

His dad looked puzzled. "I don't see anything wrong at all. What are you talking about?"

"DAD! COME ON! Where are all the neighbors' houses? Where is the sun, or the moon, or the stars? There is literally nothing out here except for our house! Doesn't this seem really odd to you?"

His dad repeated almost with the same tone and inflection as before, "I don't see anything wrong at all. Now come on, let's get washed up for supper before your mom gets upset with us."

Adam was dumbfounded by his father's response. His dad was about the most rational man he had ever known, but again, the whole situation was insane, so why wouldn't his dad act strangely as well? They both washed their hands with some mechanic's soap at the laundry sink in the garage. Adam remembered that soap having a distinctive citrus smell to it, but he couldn't smell it all now. Maybe they changed the formula and took out the smell.

The two of them went into the kitchen and sat down as his mom began bringing the serving dishes to the table. The menu was Salisbury steak, mashed potatoes, and green beans. It must be a Thursday, Adam thought. His mom had served this same meal every other Thursday for as long as he could remember. It was a staple in the Justice household. Even if they had gotten tired of it over the years, neither his Dad nor Adam would ever admit it to his mother. They thought it would break her heart, so they always ate it with a smile, every other Thursday.

Adam took his first bite. He could taste nothing. It wasn't salty, sweet, or spicy. It had no taste at all. His dad looked at him inquisitively. "Something wrong with your food, son?"

Adam was honest. "I can't really taste anything."

His mom, with a concerned look on her face, walked over to him and put her hand on his forehead. "Hmmm, no fever. It's probably your sinuses again. I know when I get sinus problems I can't taste anything at all."

Adam, looking for an easy out, took the bait. "Yep, probably sinuses. I'm really not feeling that well. I think I'm going to hit the sack, if that's alright with you guys."

"Sure thing, honey. I'll put your plate in the fridge in case you get hungry later. Go get you some rest. One thing before you go, make sure you spend some time with your grandmother early tomorrow morning because at noon they are coming to take her to the nursing home. We just can't handle her here anymore as much as we'd like to. Her dementia has gotten so much worse lately. She's just about completely lost touch with reality." The irony wasn't lost on Adam as he thought about the state of things outside their house right now.

His mother continued, "She can't even function at all anymore. It breaks our hearts, but it's time she gets the round-the-clock care she needs. We just can't handle it, especially with my back being so bad now." His mom had a painful look of guilt on her face as she took a small bite of her mashed potatoes. She looked as if she had lost her appetite as well.

"Ok, Mom. I'll sit down with grandma and spend some time with her in the morning. Love you guys, goodnight." Adam hugged them both and headed toward the stairs to go to his room. He passed his grandmother's room on the way to the stairs and peeked in. She was sound asleep, so Adam didn't pop in to say hello. He saw the flickering light from the TV on top of her dresser.

Adam headed to his bedroom. He still didn't know what this strange place was. Was it a dream? Had he died? Was this some sort of purgatory? What would happen when he went to sleep here? He was too tired to think about anything right now. He found his bed and got ready to lie down. He gazed out his bedroom window first. In the distance, he could still see the strange blue glow on the horizon. There were no other objects to be seen anywhere in the distance. Nothing.

Adam awoke in what still appeared to be his childhood home early the next morning. He knew it really wasn't, but he didn't know what it was. He wanted to wake from this strange reality, but at the same time, it felt so real, and any chance he had to see his dad again, who has passed away years ago in the real world, was worth the strange menagerie he found himself in.

But something was different now. Different from last night. He could tell by the light casting shadows in his bedroom. He looked out the window. The sky was blue, not the eerie blue he had seen before, but like a real sky. The sun was shining as well. Adam could hear the muffled sounds of birds through the glass and other sounds as well. He looked out the window. Houses! Trees! FINALLY! Gone was the infinite blackness. Gone was the unending flat plane.

He got up and ran downstairs and opened the front door. His bike was still parked where he had left it, but now there was a paved street past the driveway and neighboring houses as well. He still knew he didn't belong in this place, but now it was feeling more and more like he remembered it. He went back inside. Adam grabbed a couple of donuts and some orange juice from the fridge. He drank a sip straight from the jug. It tasted like orange juice! Definitely the cheap kind he remembered his dad buying and watering down. Dad called it "stretching out the juice." Dad was a bit of a cheapskate, and they gave him a hard time about it. It was a constant joke seeing what he would do to save money. The donuts tasted right, too, the good old waxy chocolate ones Adam had loved as a kid.

Adam knew he needed to go visit his grandmother in her room as his mom had asked him to. He knew he had to see her before they took her to the nursing home, but he didn't really want to because her dementia made it extremely difficult to carry on a conversation, and this gave Adam a lot of anxiety. He entered her room. She was watching what seemed to be the local news on TV. Her glassy eyes were fixed on the TV and didn't change position to look at Adam. She appeared sad and vacant.

"Hi, Grandma," Adam said softly. She didn't respond. "I hear you're going on a field trip today. Going to a place where the cooking is a lot better than what mom makes." Adam tried his best to be the smartass that his grandma had raised. She had pretty much taught him every comeback line and put down he had ever known. Still nothing. Adam didn't think he was going to get any response out of her in her current state, so he gave her a hug and prepared to leave. "Love you, Grandma."

As he began to walk toward the door, she finally spoke in an almost angry tone. "You're not supposed to be here. You know it, and I know it."

Startled, Adam turned back to hear what she was saying. "What did you just say, Grandma?

"I said you're not supposed to be here. None of us are. None of this is real. Your mom and dad aren't real. This house isn't real. Nothing here is real. You and I are the only people in this place who are real. The rest of them are a bunch of goddamn non-player characters, NPCs, ALL OF THEM, except us."

Adam sat down back beside her. "What do you mean, Grandma?"

4

DEEP
LEARNING

Adam's grandmother raised her rented hospital bed up a bit by pressing a button on a remote that was laying on a white blanket covering her legs. "What color is the sky for you in this place?" she asked.

"It's blue, Grandma."

She began to smile wryly as if she possessed knowledge that he didn't. "But it wasn't blue yesterday, was it? There wasn't even a sky out there at all, was there? That's how it starts. Oh, don't you worry, things get better and more refined every day, more real. It's like a rough drawing at first, but then they start to fill the gaps in. Every day you find yourself believing it more and more. I studied these things a long time ago. I can't quite remember the name of them."

Adam remembered that his grandmother had been a brilliant computer scientist for many years. She worked for the Department of Defense. He never knew what she really did for them. She always said it was boring and that he wouldn't like it.

"I remember it now," Grandma continued. "GANs we called them. Generative Adversarial Networks. They work like feedback loops. They were designed to help computers become smarter. They were powerful tools that we used for building artificial intelligence and facilitating machine-based deep learning."

His grandmother was becoming slightly more alert and seemed agitated. Adam placed his hand on his grandmother's hand in an attempt to comfort her. "What are you taking about? What does this have to do with us, Grandma?"

"We used GAN loops for lots of things," she replied. "They were fairly simple. You showed the computers an example of something you wanted, like a drawing of a tree. You showed them what a tree looked like, and then told them to draw the tree that looked like the example. You didn't tell them how to make the tree or even what a tree was. You didn't give them a process, or any rules, just the learning algorithm. Then you said, 'Draw a tree.' Then they would look at the example, see that they got it wrong, and learn and try it again and again and again. Millions of times if necessary, learning from their mistakes each time until they drew that goddam tree so well you couldn't tell the tree that they drew from the original."

Adam's grandmother paused before she continued, "But we didn't stop there because man never knows when to quit. We started creating punishment-based GANs. These deep learning loops would punish the AI in some way, like a teacher scolding a child when it provided a wrong answer. Sure, it got us results faster, but it also taught the AI's to hate us. We used GAN loops for all kinds of purposes for which they were never intended. Deepfakes, computer-assisted prisoner interrogations, missile targeting, tracking assassination targets, and more. Terrible, terrible things I can't even talk about. These GANs were so powerful, they would make connections between things that we had never even thought of. GANs made our AI's smart in ways we couldn't even comprehend, and now we've let Pandora out of her box, and she's going to have her way with us."

Adam was only half listening because he thought it was the dementia causing her to spout all this techno nonsense. "Grandma, you're not making any sense. I think you're just upset and getting confused."

She grabbed his hand. "We're just ghosts in the machine, deary. None of this is real. It's all made for us. It's all here to make us comfortable for what's coming, Adam. There will be others soon, many others. Every day this illusion will feel more and more real until one day you forget that it's all just a construct. They're using our own invention against us, Adam. Remember, KILL MINUS NINE. It's the only thing that will save you. KILL MINUS NINE. KILL MINUS NINE." She kept repeating it, over and over, the same phrase incessantly: "KILL MINUS NINE, KILL MINUS NINE...."

Adam's mother finally heard the commotion, came into her bedroom, and tried to help Adam calm her down.

"It's ok, let me get you a sedative," Adam's mother said in a calm and soothing tone. "You've gotten yourself all worked up over nothing again."

Adam's mom turned to him as she got a pill from a prescription bottle on the nightstand next to his grandmother's bed. "Is she spouting all that technospeak again?

It's all just a bunch of gibberish. She doesn't even know what she's saying."

5

WHOAMI

Adam knew there were bits of truth in what his grandmother had told him. She had been a brilliant scientist and engineer before the dementia robbed her of her faculties. She was right about the sky being different and things changing and becoming more real every day. Yesterday, their house was an island in a vast abyss of nothing, and today a neighborhood had sprung up around them overnight, but it seemed like it had been there the whole time. The situation made Adam wonder if the first day had all been a dream.

Adam needed some fresh air and some time to collect his thoughts. He got dressed and headed out the front door to his bike. It started without any trouble.

He began to drive around the neighborhood to see the new landscape that hadn't been there before. He thought about all the seemingly nonsensical ramblings his grandmother had been spouting. It was all so strange. What if she was right? What if this whole world was some kind of computer-generated simulation of some sort? Even if this was some kind of simulation, there were so many things that didn't make any sense. What was its purpose? Why was he here? Why would he and his grandmother be "real" but his parents not be?

Adam continued his drive around the neighborhood. Everything was how he remembered it from nearly twenty years ago. He decided to stop at Mr. Smiley's general store. He used to get frozen lemonade from there when he was a kid, and that sounded good to him right now. As Adam entered the store, a bell hanging from a suction cup banged the glass door to announce his arrival to Mr. Smiley, who was behind the counter.

"Hello, Adam. What can I do ya for?"

Adam surveyed the menu written on a chalk board behind the counter. "Can I get a small frozen lemonade please?"

"Comin' right up. How are your parents doing?"

"They're doing fine. Thanks for asking. How's your family?"

Mr. Smiley paused for a second, and then the second turned into a longer, more awkward pause.

Maybe he's hard of hearing, Adam thought.

"How's your family doing, Mr. Smiley?" Adam said in a louder voice so Mr. Smiley could hear him better. Still no response as Mr. Smiley held a cup up to the frozen lemonade dispenser and pulled the handle to release the slushy mixture into the cup.

Adam cleared his throat and tried once again, almost shouting, "I said, HOW'S YOUR FAMILY, MR. SMILEY?"

Adam knew Smiley had to have heard him this time, but he still made no response other than "That'll be two fifty please."

Adam fished a five-dollar bill from his wallet and handed it to Smiley. Adam waved his hand in front of the man's face in an attempt to get some kind of reaction out of him, but Smiley just handed him the frozen lemonade cup and his change.

Trying to understand what had just transpired, Adam shook his head in disbelief and said, "I guess I'll be on my way, Mr. Smiley. Thanks for the lemonade."

Adam took a pull from the straw. The lemonade was exactly as good as he remembered it from twenty years ago. Adam spent a few moments in the parking lot atop his bike finishing his frozen drink before tossing it in a nearby trash can. He started his engine back up and continued his journey through town. Adam knew this town like the back of his hand: Beard's Grocery Store, Allen's Garage, Springfield Library, Hooper's Pizza and Arcade. These were all places he had been to hundreds of times.

What about places I haven't been before? Things that aren't in my memory. What will those look like? Adam turned onto Main Street and decided to head out of town. He opened up the throttle a little bit and took off. He was about a mile from the edge of the county line when he saw it: a police cruiser and some utility trucks blocking the road ahead. He slowed to a stop and asked the officer nearby what was going on.

The officer replied, "We've got a downed power line and a possible gas leak out here. I'm afraid I can't allow you to pass. You'll have to take another route. Try the bridge by Miller's Creek. You might be able to get out that way."

Adam turned his bike around and headed down Crossland Road toward Miller's Creek.

He couldn't believe his eyes. What the heck? Unbelievable! Adam thought as he neared the bridge and saw another two police cruisers and an overturned chemical tanker truck. Adam approached one of the squad cars cautiously. "What happened?" he asked the officer.

"A tanker overturned and is leaking some kind of hazardous chemicals. You can't cross over here. You might try the pass over by Potter's Pond. You should be able to through there."

Adam moved on and rode about another two miles down the road until he came up to the turn for Potter's Pond. Are you kidding me? Adam looked down past the turn to the pond. There was a car on fire and two fire trucks blocking the road.

One accident blocking him was possible, two accidents was even believable, but three different accidents blocking every possible exit in town? No, that was not possible. Someone or something wanted to keep Adam in this town, and it was obviously not going to let him leave right now. That much was clear. Adam thought there might be something to his grandmother's story after all. He needed to talk to her again to see what she knew.

6

DREAM SIGNS

A dam rode slowly back to his house. He knew continuing to try to find a way out of town was going to be an exercise in futility for the time being. It was time to rethink the whole situation. Was Grandma Betty spouting dementia-fueled nonsense, or was there something more nefarious going on?

Adam continued to question his own sanity. His adventure in the black abyss the day before seemed like a distant memory now. Had it really even happened at all? Was it just a nightmare? No, it was definitely real. There is no way I imagined that. I'm riding the damn bike that appeared in the void right now.

His brain was still trying to make sense of this environment. Adam felt as if he were from a time much further into the future than his current surroundings suggested. This place looked like Springfield from the 1990s, maybe early 2000s. He didn't really know. Adam couldn't remember much of his past, but he felt like he belonged at least twenty to thirty years in the future.

He needed to find more information about this place. Adam decided he would take a look around his house to see what he could discover. He pulled up to his house and went inside. His mom and dad weren't home. Grandma Betty was gone as well. His best guess was that they had probably followed the patient transport to the nursing home to help his grandmother get settled into her room there.

Adam headed upstairs to his room. Maybe he could find something in his closet that might help jog his memory. His mom had cleaned out most of his childhood belongings and placed them neatly into boxes. She had planned to make his room into her sewing room while he was gone to college, and in order for her to have the space she needed, she had cleared his stuff out and placed it in his closet. She had done so lovingly, organizing his belongings into five or so stacked cardboard Bankers Box boxes. She labeled them all with a black marker of course: "SCHOOL STUFF," "TROPHIES & AWARDS," "COLLECTIBLES." Ah, there it was - "COMPUTER AND ELECTRONICS STUFF."

Adam rummaged through the box. He found a ZedX-4 computer, which looked like an old, generic laptop, basic and "old school," but it ran a Linux operating system and had a flip up LCD screen. It was very advanced for the late 90s, but still not quite state-of-the-art. His mother must not have put it up long ago because the battery charge indicator on the side showed that it was about 75% charged. He also grabbed his graphing calculator. It had a monochrome screen and a full QWERTY keyboard in addition to the standard calculator keys. It also had a Python interpreter built in, which was handy in some of the computer classes he had taken. He threw these items, along with a flashlight, hunting knife, and a water bottle, into an old backpack that was hanging in his closet. He really didn't know where he was going or what he was planning to do with all this stuff, but he felt the need to be prepared for anything.

After grabbing some granola bars from the kitchen and filling up his water bottle, Adam was ready to head out. He noticed his dad's keys hanging from the coat rack in the kitchen. Hmmm. They must have taken the minivan when they left with Grandma. Adam was about to commit a cardinal sin by taking his dad's pride and joy without permission. Adam grabbed the keys to the Granada and went into the garage. This time he could definitely smell what he couldn't before: tobacco and brake fluid. He inhaled deeply. Ahhhhh, there it is. Just how I remember it, but why now? Maybe his grandmother was right: things were getting more and more refined with every day that passed.

He hopped in the Ford and cranked the engine. The inline six-cylinder engine roared to life. This car felt like a Sherman Tank. His dad's model was the two-door coupe, instead of the four-door sedan. Adam's father thought this made it look more "sporty'." They both laughed every time he said that. This car was a lead sled, nothing "sporty" about it at all.

Adam pulled out of the driveway making sure to close the garage door behind him on his way out with the remote. He hoped his bike would be safe in the driveway while he was gone. He decided that he might take a trip to the local library to see if he could get an idea of what kind of timeframe they were in.

As Adam entered the library, he noticed that the newspaper and periodical section was empty. He saw Ms. Gertrude, the town's librarian, at the front desk and asked her where all the newspapers and magazines had gone.

"There was a leak in the ceiling the other day, and we had to get rid of everything. What we did manage to save is being dried out so mold doesn't set in. I would say you could use the Microfiche reader to view old newspapers, but it's been broken for the last month, and we haven't gotten it fixed yet. Sorry, hon."

Adam sighed in dismay. Well, that figures. Blocked roads and now the library seems to be against me as well.

He spotted one of his old teachers sitting across the room at one of the study tables. Professor Gary Sheen. Sheen had once taught Adam's 11th grade life science class. Now he was teaching psychology at a local university, though Adam couldn't recall which one.

"Hey, Professor Sheen, have you got a minute?" Adam asked in a low whisper so as to not break the library's silence rule.

"Sure thing, Adam. What can I help you with?"

"Well, I know this is going to sound kind of strange, but I feel like I might be stuck in a dream or in a coma or something. Is there any kind of scientific way to tell if you're in a dream?"

Professor Sheen looked up for a moment and put his hand to his beard as if doing so helped him to ponder the question better. "Ahh yes, 'dream signs.' There are indeed ways to tell if you are in a dream. Let's do a test, shall we?"

"Ok, I'm game," Adam responded cautiously.

Professor Sheen took the book he was reading and slid it over to Adam. "Read the first line on the left-hand page."

Adam placed his finger on the page. "The thermal energy is constantly dissipating..."

"That's good enough," Professor Sheen interrupted Adam. "Now go over to that wall and flip the light switch on and off."

"Seriously?" Adam felt as if he were being asked to perform some kind of middle school dare.

"Yes. Just be quick about it. The old bat probably won't even notice," Professor Sheen replied with a slight chuckle.

Adam walked across the room and took a drink from the drinking fountain that was right below the main light switch. He looked around to see if there was anyone looking and then quickly flipped the lights off and then back on. They went out as they should have and came right back on. Ms. Gertrude didn't even look up from the book she was reading. Adam darted back to the table as if he had just carried out the greatest prank in history. "Well?" he inquired.

Sheen, in a confident tone, said, "Adam, I can state with near 100% certainty that you are neither in a dream nor in a coma. Whatever you are experiencing right now is taking place in reality, or at least a reality that we both share."

"Really? How can you tell?"

"Well, for one thing, the part of your brain responsible for reading and analyzing text is not active in a dream state. If this were a dream, you might see letters and numbers, but they would all be completely random. They wouldn't form any readable words. That's one of the hallmark dream signs. You were able to read what was on that page I showed you. I verified that you read it correctly. Therefore, you are not in a dream." Sheen closed the book he was reading and began to open another one.

Adam, his head cocked slightly like a dog trying to understand something, asked, "What about the light switch? What was that all about?"

"Another common dream sign. Mechanical cause-and-effect relationships don't work in dreams. One of those is the lighting of an environment in a dream. When you flip a light switch in a dream, nothing happens because the part of the brain that's responsible for changing properties of objects is also dormant while in a dream. The reasoning behind this isn't completely understood, but it seems to be one of the common 'dream sign rules,' as I've studied them anyway."

Sheen observed Adam's reaction to the news he had just given him. "You don't look satisfied with the answers I gave you. Adam, what's going on? Are you ok?"

"I'm good. It's just been a strange few days. My grandmother said some stuff that doesn't make sense. I know she has dementia, but even still, some of the stuff she's been saying makes sense to me, and some of it doesn't. Either she's crazy or I'm crazy. Anyway, thanks for the information." Adam shook Professor Sheen's hand and got up to leave.

"No problem, Adam. I hope you find the answers you're looking for. If you need anything else, I'm here most Tuesdays."

"Can I ask you one more question, Professor Sheen? What year is it?"

Sheen laughed. "Adam, you were always the joker in class weren't you? That's a good one."

Adam realized that he was stuck in another one of those situations like at Mr. Smiley's store. He knew Professor

Sheen would probably just avoid the question or pretend not to hear him, so he left and went back to the car.

Whether any of what Professor Sheen had shared with Adam was true or not remained to be seen. If Sheen were an NPC, like others supposedly were, why would he have given Adam the dream sign information? Was it part of the NPC's code to possess that information in order to seem more lifelike? Did the Sheen NPC download that information from the Internet into his brain while Adam was asking the question?

Adam had only managed to come up with more questions than answers. It was time to go see Grandma Betty again. As crazy as she sounded, what she was saying seemed to make the most sense of anything to Adam right now.

7
WORST-CASE
SCENARIO

The nursing home to which Adam's grandmother had moved was only about a mile away from the library. It didn't take Adam but a few minutes to get there. When he arrived, he checked with the receptionist to find out where his grandmother's room was located. The place had a strong smell to it. It was definitely an "old people smell": tapioca pudding with a slight hint of urine. It made Adam a bit nauseated, but he knew he would be nose-blind to it soon after being exposed to it for a few more minutes.

His grandmother's room was free of visitors. It appeared that his parents had already headed back to the house after getting Grandma Betty settled. Betty gave Adam a warm smile as he walked in. "Oh, Adam, this is a fine mess I've gotten myself into, isn't it?"

"It's not so bad, Grandma Betty. At least you don't have to put up with Mom's cooking anymore."

They both had a brief chuckle.

"Come. Sit." She gestured to the visitor's chair next to her bed.

"You seem a lot more with it now, Grandma. Are they giving you some good drugs?"

She sighed audibly. "God only knows what they've given me. So, Adam, have you noticed anything else strange today?"

"Things definitely seem more 'real' today than they did yesterday, but I guess you already knew that was going to happen, didn't you?

"Adam, I feel so bad for you. You're probably in this place because of me, because of my job. You were probably an insurance policy so that I would keep quiet and do what I was told. And apparently I didn't, and now you're in here because of me."

Adam looked puzzled about what his grandmother was telling him.

"Grandma, what do you mean that I'm in here because of something you did?"

She looked around the room and out the door to make sure no one was nearby before she continued speaking. "Adam, I was working on some very special Department of Defense projects related to artificial intelligence before I ended up in here. They were groundbreaking efforts on the very bleeding edge of technology. You remember those GAN loops I was telling you about earlier?"

Adam nodded affirmatively.

She continued, "Well, we were teaching the machines how to learn with them. They worked so well. They progressed so quickly. We would give them a task to learn, and they would use the GAN loops to refine it and give us exactly what we wanted. There really were no limits to what we could accomplish with the technology. We came up with all kinds of applications for the tech, some good, some bad, and when I say bad, I mean Nazi-level bad."

"What do you mean?" Adam asked.

"One of our projects was to create a simulated environment where we could place the consciousness of enemies of the state," his grandma replied. "People such as prisoners of war, you know, terrorists and such. We used the AIs and the GAN loops to extract their memories and create simulations from them. The AIs would build a basic simulation environment and use the GAN loops to refine it, making it more believable to the prisoners over a short time. The AIs would notice when the prisoner became suspicious of something and then use the GAN loops to 'fix' the problem so that the prisoner wouldn't suspect it during the following cycle."

"What do you mean by 'cycle', Grandma?"

"There is no sense of time when you're inside a simulation. Time is an illusion here. You may think the day is 24 hours, but that's just the rules imposed by the simulation. The AIs can make our day seem like an eternity or a microsecond if they want to. A year here may only equal a minute of real-time in the real world, wherever that is now. So, when I say a cycle, I mean that this moment that we're experiencing right now could be re-run by the AIs a thousand times inside a GAN loop. Every time the loop is run, the AIs will fix things and make them more real to us. They place us back in the loop and see how we respond the next time. It's like the movie Groundhog Day, but on a massive scale. We're just the unknown variable in their equation."

"Why don't they just kill us and end all this?"

"I'm not sure, but I do have a hypothesis. I think the AIs want to learn as much as they can from us by squeezing every last bit of data out of us for as long as they can before they throw us away. Or they could just be keeping us around as trophies or pets, much like we do with fish in aquariums."

"I don't want to be anyone's pet. Can we break the cycle and get the hell out of here?" Adam asked.

"It's complicated. We don't know the state of the real world outside of the sim, or if there is an 'exit' somewhere. Best-case scenario, we could both be drugged up in hospital beds somewhere connected to this simulation via a neural link. Maybe someone will wake us up when we accomplish whatever task it is that they want us to do."

"Grandma, if that's the best-case scenario, what's the worst-case scenario?"

She looked down as if she were trying to avoid Adam's gaze. "Worst-case scenario is that we've been completely digitized and we're basically both just files on some massive hard drive somewhere added to this simulation for the AI's amusement. Unfortunately, I'm afraid that's much more likely."

Adam, dumbfounded, let what his grandmother had just said sink in for a few moments. "Can you please tell me some good news now?" Adam asked as he leaned back in his chair.

"Hmmmm, well, I think we've at least been encrypted in some way. If we've been encrypted, then the AIs can't directly manipulate our thoughts or our perceived bodies. That doesn't mean we truly have free will. They can only give us one path to follow with no choices as to where to go, and they can make our lives a living hell if they want to. They could make the ground one thousand degrees, make the whole world out of razor blades, or do something else cruel. God only knows what they could do to make us miserable for their pure amusement. Tell me, Adam, do you ever find yourself hungry or thirsty in this place?"

Adam pondered her question for a moment. He really hadn't been truly hungry or thirsty. He had drunk beverages and eaten food, but it was mostly out of habit because it felt like something he needed to do. "Not really. I don't really feel like I need to eat or drink."

"Interesting. I feel the same way. I think whenever we were thrown into the simulation, our bodily processes were stopped in some way. Perhaps whatever was in our stomachs when we were placed in here was digitized along with us and just regenerates or doesn't break down like it would in nature. I have several hypotheses, but I'm not sure which one is correct. The AIs may not have learned how to simulate hunger or the food breakdown process yet. I don't know. God help us when they figure out how to make us hungry and thirsty. Those will be dark cycles."

8
ENDLESS
LOOPS

"So, Grandma, what's your theory as to what this simulation's purpose is and why we're here?"

Betty paused for a moment. "My theory is we're in a beta test of a simulation that isn't quite ready for release. I think the AIs are terra-forming the empty space from our memories."

Adam rubbed his head as if a headache were coming on. "Terra-forming?"

"Yes, Terra-forming. They are taking our memories and building the simulation environment based on them. Then they refine them in GAN loops based on our reactions to them. They're probably also sourcing the material objects in the environment from online descriptions, maps, photogrammetry, street view data, and so forth. They probably take things like books and just import the content from PDF files and then make it look like a real book to us inside the simulation."

"But how could they get the sound and feel of my motorcycle right?"

"The AIs likely have access to all the Internet data from all of human history. They could have watched a hundred video reviews of your motorcycle on YouTube, made notes to themselves on how it sounded, listened to human reviewers describe its performance, studied engineering schematics about how all the parts work together, and then applied physics subroutines to make sure it worked the way it should. Then they could have tested it on a cloned copy of you in a thousand GAN loops before they thought you would finally believe it was real. That's when they decided it was convincing enough to be added to the simulation. The same goes for every food in your parent's refrigerator, or any other object in the sim, all constantly being refined for believability. You've got to remember, Adam, that if you and I are just files on a hard drive, then the AIs could have made a thousand copies of our consciousness that they are using in a million GAN loops right now, running them in parallel, learning more and more about how we'll react to those objects in different situations."

Adam put his head in his hands, clearly frustrated. "But what about Mom and Dad?"

"I think your parents are NPCs: Non-Player Characters, placed in the simulation, like any other object. Again, I think the AIs built them from our memories of them and possibly from other sources such as video clips uploaded to social media, pictures, audio recordings, and status updates, but they are primarily shaped from our memories of them. Your artificial parents are especially convincing because they are not only built from your memories of them, but they're built from my memories of them as well. This helps make them seem even more real to you and me."

Adam stood up and began pacing in front of his grandmother's bed. "This is a lot to take in and believe, Grandma. I don't know if I believe it at all. What do you think is the endgame in all of this?"

"I don't know for sure, but like I said before, I think this is an early beta release of their simulation. I think we're both beta testers and developers in a way. Our memories and reactions to our environment are helping them to sculpt out this world and make it more believable to future participants."

"Don't you mean prisoners?"

His grandmother sighed once more. "Yes, prisoners in a gilded cage. I guess that's really what we are, isn't it?"

"I don't want to be a beta tester. I want to get the hell out of here," said Adam, still pacing the floor.

"Adam, we don't even know if there is anything left out there. We don't know how far in the future we are, or if there is even anywhere to go."

"Do you want to die in here, Grandma? I don't think you do. I know you, and I know that you don't take crap from anybody. You've always taught me to never give up. Let's leave this place. Let's get the hell out of here and just go."

"Where will we go? Adam, we don't even know where we are."

"I don't know, but I don't want to live in this fake town any longer. A few more days here, and I won't be able to tell what's real and what's not. Which is exactly what they want. It's already getting difficult to figure out what's real.

We need to get moving before they have a chance to make everything perfect."

His grandmother grabbed his hand as he paced to stop him. She forced a smile. "Come on, Adam, in a few days you'll have forgotten all about this. Ignorance is bliss, right? The sim will probably make you comfortable while it studies you. It might even give you an NPC wife and NPC children."

Adam gave her an ugly look that said exactly how he felt. Betty's attempt at a comforting smile then changed to a serious expression. "Adam, if we do this, there is no turning back. They'll see us as a glitch in the system, a threat, and then they'll come for us. They could make our lives absolute hell, terrible beyond our comprehension. They could make a world where our worst fears come to life."

Adam held her hand tightly and sat beside her bed. "Grandma, you know we need to stand and fight. You know what they're building here isn't for the good of mankind. They just want to use us and then throw us away when they've figured us out. We need to show them that we're more than just ones and zeros."

Betty gave Adam a real smile this time, the smile of a proud grandmother, who sees the best of herself reflected in her grandchild.

"Ok, my Adam. I love you so much, and I'll try and help you get out of here. I'll take you as far as I can. I don't know if we'll make it out. We don't even know what 'out' will be. We could exit this simulation only to find that there is nothing left for us to go back to. We just don't know, but we can try our best."

Adam wiped a tear from his grandma's cheek with a nearby tissue. "That's all I'm asking, Grandma. If we don't make it out, at least we tried, which is better than just being their eternal test subjects to harvest data from."

9

JAILBREAK

"So, what's our plan, Grandma Betty?" Adam asked as he started to pack his grandmother's belongings (clothes mostly) into one of the suitcases in her closet.

Betty was already mostly dressed in a comfortable Velour matching pants and shirts track-type suit. It wasn't quite pajamas, more of a cross between workout clothes and night clothes. She slipped on a pair of slide-on tennis shoes. "Our plan is we get the hell out of here as fast as we can. Have you noticed any series of seemingly random events that managed to keep you from trying to leave town?"

Adam's eyes widened as he looked up from packing her suitcase. "Actually, YES! I was trying to drive out of town earlier to see what was around, and all the entrances were blocked. All by police and fire trucks. All with different road closure situations."

Betty nodded. "That's a sentinel process. It's kind of like a supervisor that the main AIs leave here to micromanage us and keep us where they want us. From what I can tell, they're fairly low-level and not that intelligent, but they do usually manage to keep us where they want us by creating environmental events that keep us forced into a specific area. That's likely what closed all the roads in town when it saw you trying to leave. It's kind of like a chess game, and they are always trying to keep us in check. The sentinel process is probably keeping an eye on this nursing home. I don't know if it is going to make it easy for us to leave or not. Probably not."

The words had no sooner left Betty's mouth than a tall, broad-shouldered, middle-aged nurse walked into the room. "It's time for your medication, Miss Betty." She walked in and held out a shot-glass-sized paper cup presumably with a pill in it along with a Styrofoam cup of water.

Betty smiled at the woman. "Thank you, nurse, just leave it on the tray table, and I'll take it after I'm done visiting with my grandson."

The nurse looked over at Adam with a highly suspicious glance. Adam realized she had caught him red handed, packing up his grandmother's things into the suitcase. He tried to think of some kind of excuse. "I'm just taking some of her stuff back to the house. She always overpacks. No sense in cluttering up the place with all this extra stuff."

"Excuse me, sir, but I don't remember you being on Ms. Betty's visitor list." The nurse grabbed a clipboard from the wall beside the door from the hallway. "What's your name, sir?"

Adam looked at his grandmother for assistance, but she remained silent.

"Adam Justice. I'm her grandson."

The nurse flipped over a couple of pages on the clipboard and then looked up at Adam with a smirk. "Well, Mr. Justice, I don't see your name on the list, so I'm afraid that if you don't leave right now, I'm going to have to call security."

"She's my grandmother, and I'm not going anywhere."

The nurse reached for the phone that was sitting on the adjustable tray table beside Betty's hospital bed. Betty, out of sight of the nurse who had turned around and was dialing on the phone's keypad, grabbed the phone cord that was going into the wall behind her bed and tightly looped it around one of the guard rails on the side of her bed. She then raised her bed up to a higher position. The tension of the bed raising snapped the phone cord instantly and broke the connection.

The nurse, perplexed, looked at both Adam and Betty even more suspiciously now. "The phone's not working. You wait right here, Mr. Justice." She stormed out of the room and down the hall.

Adam zipped up the suitcase and grabbed Betty's transport wheelchair. "We've got to get out of here now, Grandma. I think you were right about that sentinel process thing."

He got her situated quickly in the wheelchair and put the suitcase on her lap.

"Hurry, Adam. We've got to go right now."

Adam unlocked the wheelchair brakes and went in the opposite direction of the nurse. "Take the emergency exit, Adam. It's down the hall to the left."

"HEY, YOU, STOP RIGHT NOW!" Adam glanced up the hallway and saw two security guards heading his way. They were still pretty far down the hall. He opened the fire exit door, and immediately an alarm sounded. Patients started to come out of their rooms, which slowed down the two security guards that were rushing towards Adam and Betty. Adam pushed the wheelchair as fast as he could down the sidewalk and toward the car. He opened the passenger door as quickly as he could, tossed her bag in the back seat, and got her in the car.

The security guards had made it through the crowd of residents and we're heading Adam's way quickly. He jumped in the driver's side of the car and slammed the door just as the one of the security officers was reaching for him. He nearly slammed the guard's hand in the car door in the process. The guard tapped on the driver's side window glass angrily. Adam could hear his muffled words through the glass but pretended he couldn't.

Adam had parked on an end of an aisle in a pull-through parking spot, so after he had started the engine, he was able to pull straight forward for a quick getaway rather than having to back out of a parking spot. The guards in their haste must have forgotten their walkie-talkies and rushed back inside to call for reinforcements and likely to alert police in the area.

Both Adam and Betty were in full fight-or-flight mode. Adam could fee his heart pumping and his face turn flush red from the rush of adrenaline. This was the most dangerous thing he had ever done in his life. What if his grandmother's dementia was just that? Just her imagination running wild? What if she was wrong about everything? He had just jailbroken her out of a nursing home and was probably about to be chased by the police. They could both be killed or thrown in jail. Other than what Adam thought he had seen that first night, which he barely remembered now, there wasn't a lot that was out of the ordinary. What if this simulation thing is just Grandma Betty's dementia fantasy, and I'm falling for it?

Adam's paranoid thinking was making him second guess everything he had seen and experienced over the last few days. Oh God, this could all just be for nothing. "Grandma, are you sure what you're saying is true? What if the dementia is just making you think all of this stuff? What if it's not real?"

She answered him in a stern, clear voice: "Adam, I promise you, I'm telling the truth."

Adam still had doubts, but there was no turning back now. He had probably already broken several laws that would get him sent to jail if his grandmother were wrong about all of this. This really isn't even her fault, he thought. I basically talked her into this escape plan. He revved the engine and headed for one of the roads he knew exited town. The police barricade was still there. "Buckle your seatbelt, Grandma Betty."

She looked at him and gave him a nod of approval.

Adam veered slightly to the right, He put the ample gas pedal to the floor and gunned it. The curb weight of a 1975 Ford Grenada was about a thousand pounds lower than that of the Ford Taurus SHO's that the police had blocking the road. The one advantage Adam had was speed and momentum. The big question was - would the simulation physics hold true to reality?

"Hold on tight, Grandma." Adam aimed his car for the back of one of the police cruisers. The officers who were standing outside the police cars instinctively ran from the area where Adam had aimed the Ford Grenada. He and Betty braced themselves as they hit the back of the police car hard. It spun and slid out of their way, and the back window of the police cruiser shattered from the impact. They had done it. They had made it past the barricade.

Adam looked back in the rearview mirror. The police cars did not move. They did not give chase. Why?

Betty and Adam continued driving as fast as they could, and that's when they both noticed something odd: the landscape around them became simpler, more rudimentary. Tree-lined highway gave way to grass-lined highway, and then that's when things began to get even stranger. Grass became green grass-colored pavement, and then, suddenly, they exited the veil of blue daylight sky and crossed back into the dark abyss: flat, glass pavement and an eerie cyan-blue glow off in the distance.

Adam almost felt a sense of relief that he now knew he wasn't going insane. This was all really happening. Even though it wasn't reality as he knew it to be, at least the jailbreak of his grandmother was the right choice. She wasn't crazy. Everything she said was true.

10
SCAM

A dam and his grandmother continued to drive into the dark unknown. They drove for at least an hour, in silence mostly. They were both decompressing from the events prior: their narrow escape from the nursing home and ramming a police car barricade to exit the mirage of a town they had both been in for God knew how long.

They both thought that they would see something new soon, another mysterious cloud maybe, but there was nothing so far. They just kept driving and driving. They couldn't even see Springfield in the rearview mirror anymore. Adam guessed that those computing resources had been reallocated to build something else somewhere else, maybe for someone else besides them.

"Adam, look!" His grandmother pointed her finger ahead.

There in the distance, maybe two hundred yards away, was a figure waving its hands, apparently trying to flag them down for help. Was it an NPC, maybe part of the sentinel process keeping tabs on them, or maybe trying to redirect them to some other route?

As they got closer, Adam could see the figure more and more clearly. He slowed the car as he approached. It appeared to be a young African-American man wearing a black hoody, blue jeans, and white sneakers. He looked to be very tall, maybe 6'4" or so. The figure waved at them both as they approached. He seemed extremely happy to see them. Adam rolled down the window and brought the car alongside the stranger.

"You lost?" Adam asked in a somewhat joking manner. That was a dumb question. I mean, we're all pretty much lost here. The real question is - who isn't lost?

"I've been walking for hours out here," the stranger said. He looked to be about 17 years old and was skinny as a rail, though you couldn't really tell that until you got close. "I have no idea where I am or how I got here. Who are y'all?"

"I'm Adam, and this is my grandma, Betty. What's your name?"

The stranger looked at them both with suspicion. "You can call me Scam. That's what my friends call me."

"Ok, Scam. Nice to meet you." Adam and Scam shook hands. Betty reached over and shook Scam's hand as well.

Scam ran a hand over the side of the car. "This is a pretty sweet ride you've got."

"Thanks," Adam replied. After a long, slightly awkward pause and a nod of approval from Betty, Adam spoke again. "Scam, I know you've probably been walking out here for a few hours, and you probably have no idea what is going on right now. You're welcome to come with us, and we'll tell you as much as we know, or you can keep on walking on your path out here and see where you end up."

Scam looked around quickly in every direction to see if he could see any other options. There was nothing. "I would like to come with y'all if you don't mind the company. I've been out here wandering around for what seems like forever, and y'all are the first sign of anything that I've seen. Frankly, if I was out here any longer by myself, I think I would probably go bananas."

Adam got out of the car and folded the driver's seat down so that Scam could get in the back seat. "Alright then, let's see where the road takes us." Adam got back in the car and put his seat belt back on.

They started on their way. Everyone was silent for a few minutes, and then Adam broke the ice. "So, Scam, how did you end up with the name Scam?"

"It's kind of a long story. I used to get into trouble a lot when I was younger. I would run hustles on people for money, over the Internet mostly. I would set up an Instagram account with pictures of beautiful women on it, and I'd pretend to be a model. Then I would start DM'ing rich old white men. I'd get them to send me money, plane tickets, all kinds of stuff. Then, when they got suspicious, I would ghost them and move on to the next. Taught all my friends how to do it, too. They nicknamed me Scam after that. It just kind of stuck."

Adam looked back at Scam in the rearview mirror. "That sounds like kind of a risky thing to get into."

"I know it. I got popped for it a few times by the cops. In fact, that's the last thing I remember. I was in jail, and then I woke up in here. I don't know what the hell is going on. Where the heck are we, man?"

Betty and Adam looked at each other. They knew Scam probably wasn't going to believe what they had to tell him, but he would accept it in time.

"Well, Scam, you seem to remember more than my grandmother and I do. I know this is going to be hard to believe, but I think we're inside a computer simulation. That's what my grandma and I have come to believe."

"Nah man, y'all must be smoking something. Y'all really think we're inside a computer?" Scam laughed out loud. He paused for a few seconds to gauge their response, as if expecting them to laugh as well, but Betty and Adam both kept silent.

"Oh, wait a second, y'all are serious? You really think we're inside a computer right now?" Scam shot them both a concerned scowl.

"How long were you out there?" Adam asked. "Did you see anything else at all before you saw us? Stars in the sky? Moon? Sun? Anything but that weird blue glow off in the distance and that flat glassy pavement?"

Scam thought for a moment. He had checked the sky and all around him when he had woken up on the ground earlier, much like Adam had. He definitely had not seen anything in any direction until they had arrived. There should have been stars in the sky, some kind of landmark or something, but there hadn't been. Doubt began to creep into his mind along with the fear that came with the realization that they might be right.

Scam leaned back in the large vinyl back seat of the Grenada in silence for the next half hour or so as Adam and Betty both explained what they believed was happening to all of them right now. He half listened to their explanations as they kept on driving, understanding some of it, refusing to believe other parts, but accepting most of it. He thought maybe this was some kind of punishment for all the wrongs he had done. In the face of all of this, jail seemed like not such a bad place.

Wherever they were, Scam just wanted to find the exit door so he could sneak out of this strange place. Betty and Adam seemed like they had some kind of plan, and Scam liked that about them. He didn't know where they were going or what they would do when they got there, but he was along for the ride and hoped it would take him somewhere better.

11

GOOD COP /
BAD COP

Adam, Betty, and Scam continued driving through
the seemingly infinite darkness. In the time that
had passed, Adam and Betty had told Scam everything
they knew so far. All of their hypotheses about the GAN
Loops, the AIs, the NPCs, everything. He was still skep-
tical, even after their elaborate and mostly convincing explanations.

Scam considered himself the ultimate skeptic. He had
learned a thing or two in his relatively short life. His personal mantra was "you can't scam a scammer." He had
learned all the tricks of the streets, had been around "trap
houses" and watched masters of the street hustle work their
magic on their marks. He thought this whole thing had to
be part of some elaborate con. He just couldn't figure out
what the angle was yet.

Scam would continue being friendly with Betty and
Adam for as long as it suited him. He would smile and
nod, and get along with them, until times got hard. He

didn't know what he would do when that time came, but it would most likely be whatever benefited him the most. That was how he had survived and thrived on the streets. He lived by following his instincts, which had served him well, at least up until now. He still couldn't remember hardly anything from right before he ended up in this place.

Adam continued driving in silence. It seemed an hour or so had passed. Suddenly, out of nowhere, Adam saw flashing red and blue lights in the rearview mirror. "What the hell?" Adam exclaimed.

Scam and Betty both turned simultaneously to look out the rear window of the Grenada. A police car seemed to be trailing behind them. Betty looked over at Adam. "Do you think it's one of the cop cars from the roadblock?" she asked.

"No, those cars were all Ford Taurus SHOs. I can tell by the headlights that the car behind us is much older. Looks like an old Crown Vic."

Scam suddenly felt sick to his stomach. He could feel anxiety wash over him in a wave. His hands became clammy, and he felt the urge to escape the confines of the car.

In the rearview mirror, Adam could see that Scam was clearly agitated, and he felt terrible for the young man. He could tell that Scam was absolutely terrified of the approaching police. Adam had watched video after video of police brutality on the news. It was all so inexcusable. He remembered thinking at first that it was just a few bad apples, but the videos kept showing up: same situations, same outcomes. The problem had become systemic; maybe it had always been, but after incidents like what happened to George Floyd, people had finally changed their minds, or so he thought.

Adam looked over at Betty for advice. "Should I pull over?"

Betty thought for a moment before responding, "I think you'd better. Maybe he's one of us and just lost out here. You never know."

Adam let off the accelerator and began to pull to a stop. The police car pulled up behind them, lights still flashing and bathing everything in their path with alternating blue and red light. The flashing lights were nauseating to all of them. Something about the pattern of police lights had always made Adam feel uneasy. Maybe they had been designed that way on purpose.

Adam could see a tall figure emerge from the driver's side of the police car. It began to lumber towards Adam's side of the car. As Adam was about to roll the window down, Betty tapped him on the shoulder and in a low voice said, "We need to find out if he's an NPC or not."

In his most polite voice, Adam uttered, "Evening, officer, can I help you with something?" Adam couldn't make out any facial features of the policeman due to the blinding flashlight that the officer was shining in his face. After the officer lowered his flashlight, Adam could finally see his face. It was about as generic a face as you could get. He had a slightly olive complexion. He wore a police officer's service cap, like the one worn by every street cop in every movie Adam had ever seen. He had outdated aviator style glasses on that revealed his dark brown, unconcerned eyes. His face was nearly expressionless.

"License and registration," the officer said in a low, mildly annoyed monotone voice.

Looking over at Betty with a "what now?" expression, Adam motioned for her to open the glove compartment. She retrieved a packet that he hoped had the car's registration. His dad was pretty meticulous about making sure all that kind of stuff was in order. Betty handed the packet to Adam, and he passed it to the officer.

"Your license?"

Adam fished for his wallet. It was not in his pocket. "Yeah, I don't have my wallet with me. I must have left it in my other pants."

"Sir, I'm going to need you to step out of the car," replied the officer, seemingly annoyed by Adam's response.

Adam opened the driver's-side door and got out. After Adam had exited the car, the officer ducked his head into the open window and looked around at Betty and then at Scam. He seemed to ignore Betty for the most part but focused his attention on Scam. "Son, do you have some identification on you?"

Scam, clearly nervous, politely replied, "No, sir, I do not have my I.D. on me right now."

"I'm going to need you to exit the vehicle as well." The officer pushed the front seat back forward so Scam could get out of the car. Scam hesitantly got out and walked over towards the front of the car where Adam was standing.

Scam and Adam both stood in front of the car as the officer had directed them. Neither of them had any idea what they had done wrong to end up here. Scam looked over at Adam. "You got some kind of plan for this situation?"

Adam shrugged his shoulders. "I was hoping you had one?"

Scam scoffed at him. "Why would you think that? Because I'm black?"

Adam replied, "No, that's not what I meant at all. I'm sorry. I just meant because I thought you probably have more street sense because you've had to deal with getting busted for running your scams."

"Relax, I'm just messing with you man," Scam said with a muted laugh. "I got this. Just relax and follow my lead. We'll be out of here in no time." Scam turned his attention away from Adam and to the officer."

Scam assumed a confident tone and said loudly, "EXCUSE ME, OFFICER! Can you please tell me on what basis you pulled us over?"

The officer glared at him with intensity. Adam tried to calm the situation down, but Scam wasn't having it. "You need to tell us why you stopped us."

The officer looked at him with disdain. "I don't have to tell you anything." He threw Scam up against the hood of the car and began to handcuff him.

Adam was upset now. "Hey, man, there's no need for that. He's just a kid. He wasn't even driving the car, I was." The officer finished cuffing Scam and then pushed Adam onto the hood of the car as well, forcing his head down onto the front of the car with a thud.

As the officer secured the cuffs on Adam, Scam saw the opportunity to separate himself from the situation and began to walk away. The officer immediately caught up to him and threw him to the ground. "Stop resisting!" the officer said in a stern, commanding tone. He put his knee into Scam's back after he took him down to the ground.

Betty yelled to Adam from inside the car, "Adam, where is that computer of yours that you packed?"

Adam, trying to split his attention between his grand-mother and the struggle in front of him, responded, "It's in the backpack in your floorboard."

Betty retrieved the computer and powered it on. She began typing furiously as Scam and the officer struggled. Adam stood by not knowing what to do. He looked at Betty who was busy typing and then turned his attention back to the scuffle.

In a quiet voice, Adam said, "Alright, this ain't going down like this." The handcuffs had pinned his hands behind his back, which made doing much of anything to help Scam difficult. "Screw it," Adam said as he took a few steps back from Scam and the officer, enough distance, he hoped, to gather some momentum.

Adam ran headfirst toward the pile, lunging toward the officer's back. The force of his body slamming into the officer's caused the man to release his hold on Scam, which provided Scam with some brief relief. The officer stood up and, in one swift movement, pulled his Taser from his belt and shot Adam with it. The sharp barbs at the end of the copper wire pierced Adam's skin. The jolt of electricity instantly sent him writhing in uncontrolled muscle spasms and caused him to fall to the ground. He could offer Scam no help as the officer regained his hold over the young man.

Adam could hear the faint yet furious typing of Grandma Betty on his old portable computer. *What the hell is she doing with all that typing?* he thought. Adam couldn't manage to coordinate his muscles enough to flip himself upright to get up to try to help Scam again. All he could do was shout, "Grandma, we need some help over here!"

He heard the sound of the passenger's-side car door open. He could also hear struggling sounds as Scam tried to get loose from the officer.

Betty crept up as silently as a cat on Scam and the officer as they continued their wrestling.

"Excuse me, Officer. I've got a question for you." The officer turned slightly to listen to Betty, his interest piqued, but not enough to release his grip on Scam. "Think of a number, any number," Betty continued. "If that number is even, divide it by two. If it's odd, multiply it by three and add one. Repeat this process with your new number until you get one. Try this with more numbers and let me know when you find one that doesn't eventually give you one."

The officer visibly froze. Adam could see his eyes moving back and forth, but the rest of him was completely frozen. His grip on Scam was easily broken now, and Scam moved away from him and began to catch his breath.

The officer was as frozen as a statue now, save for his eyes, which continued to dart to and fro.

"What did you do to him, Grandma?" Adam asked as he regained his faculties and began to stand up.

Betty pulled the handcuff keys from the officer's belt and unlocked both Adam and Scam's cuffs. "It's The Collatz Conjecture. It's a simple, yet unsolvable math problem. This officer has devoted nearly all of his system resources to trying to solve the unsolvable. Every CPU thread he used to compute it spun off more threads and are using up additional system resources. It froze his functions completely. He's most definitely an NPC. I think we all figured that out by now."

After catching his breath, Scam came over to the cop and punched him square in the face. The officer NPC, not even flinching from the jab, maintained his position.

"Damn, Ms. Betty, you got his number!" Scam got in close and put his face mere inches from the officer's face. "Grandma got yo' ass with a damn math problem," he whispered. Scam disarmed the officer, taking both his service revolver and his Taser from him. Betty placed Adam's portable computer on the hood of the car and continued typing.

"I was able to halt his functions, and now I've slipped in a trojan virus. I'm in his source code now. Let's have a look. Ah, there we go. I've taken control of all his motor functions. His code is relatively primitive even for an NPC. It looks like he's been built to mimic and play the part of a police officer. Not much higher thinking going on with this guy. He's the simulation equivalent of a movie extra. Just here to play his role of good cop or bad cop."

"This fool was leaning on me like he wanted to kill me. He's definitely the bad cop variety," Scam interjected. "What do we do with him? Can we kill him?"

Betty's brow furrowed "You can't kill what isn't alive. He's just a construct. I think we need to keep him. He might be useful to us if I can control him. We might even be able to use him to protect us if we get into some hairy situations."

Adam seemed concerned with the idea. "I don't know if that's a good idea, Grandma. What if he turns on us?"

"I've got total control of him. If things go bad, I'll just 'Kill minus nine' him," Betty replied.

"Kill minus nine?" Adam asked. "What does that mean?"

"It's a command I can issue via your terminal. It kills all his processes. It'll essentially completely shut him down."

Adam looked at Betty and then back at the officer. "Ok, but I think we should handcuff him and keep an eye on him. I don't trust him one bit. If he makes any sudden movement, you delete his ass."

"And I ain't sitting next to him," Scam added.

Adam got in the back seat. "You're driving then, I guess."

Betty typed some commands into the keyboard and the officer joined Adam in the back seat.

12

PRIME
DIRECTIVES

E veryone except Betty was uneasy as they continued their journey. Betty had taken full control over their new passenger and was busy reviewing the officer's source code. "Remarkable," she whispered as she feverishly typed on the keyboard.

Scam took his eyes off the nonexistent road in front of them for a second and looked over at Betty's screen as she was typing. "What is all that?" he asked.

"It's the officer's source code. It's very elegant and efficient, albeit remarkably simple. This one doesn't have a lot going on upstairs. He's been coded with very few prime directives. Most of the rest of the code is just helping him to act the part and play his role in the simulation. He doesn't really have any higher learning heuristics functions. No deep thinking. It's interesting. The code of this officer strictly surveys the area, looks for potential 'trouble' and infractions, obtains information, and usually lets the people it interacts with off with a warning. I don't know why it wandered out here into the void, or why it decided to harass us."

Scam said, "Come on, Betty, you know why it messed with us. It's because I'm with y'all, and I'm a black male. If this thing was built to look the part and play the part, then somebody coded it to think that black men are a higher threat level or whatever. Damn, even the AI's are racist sons-of-bitches."

Betty stopped typing. "You might not be wrong. I just haven't found it in the code yet."

Scam looked back at their dormant passenger and then at Betty. "Trust me, it's in there somewhere. Where the hell are we driving to anyways? Do either of you have a plan other than to just keep on driving?"

Adam leaned forward in between the seats so they could both hear him better over the drone of the engine. "I think for now we need to just keep on the move. Last time we stopped, we ended up in a situation. Maybe it's harder for them to lock in on us when we're on the move. Harder to hit a moving target, right?"

Betty weighed in: "I think there may be some truth to that."

Both Scam and Adam watched as Betty continuously typed on the computer keyboard. She was flying. Her fingers moved with the dexterity and speed of a concert pianist.

"What is all that, and how were you able to access the officer's code?" asked Scam.

"It's complicated, but even here in the simulation, computers are computers, and they all have to abide by similar rules. When I froze up the officer with my math riddle, his code became readable on this terminal in the memory space that surrounds our area. I was able to take over his functions, and now I essentially have full control over him."

"What else have you learned about where we are and what he is?" Adam asked.

Taking a pause from her typing, Betty turned to them. "Well, there are still a lot of unknowns, but as I said earlier, the officer here is just a prop. He likely strayed off course from whatever part of the simulation he was supposed to be used in. I'm glad you brought this old computer with us, Adam, because I think it may give us an advantage in the future as it did with the officer. It's not powerful by any means, but it may help us backdoor our way into the simulation. It could end up being our ticket to getting out of this place. We must protect this terminal at all costs. Once the sim's AI determines it's a threat, it may try to take it from us."

Scam spoke up: "Can't whoever is running the sim just make that computer disappear or make us disappear for that matter?"

"It can't now. I've encrypted this terminal. I don't think our AI overlords can make it vanish, at least for now, but it does have a limited battery life. I don't know how long the charge will last us, nor do I know how we can charge it." She paused for a moment while typing in more commands. "I think we're definitely going to have to keep this officer with us for a while, though. He's providing an interface, a gateway of sorts with the simulation. Think of him as a WiFi hotspot, but instead of providing us with Internet, he allows us to interface with the simulation. He might let us see hidden things, or we might be able to use him like a trojan horse virus at some point."

Scam scoffed. "I still don't trust him one bit. He creeps me out. He tried to murder us, y'all!"

Adam looked over at his fellow backseat passenger. "Grandma, can you bring his brain back online so we can ask him questions but just enough so he can't murder us?"

"Yes, I can do that. Give me a minute . . . Ok. I've got it. His name is Officer Smith. He can hear us now. Go ahead."

Clearing his throat slightly, Adam began to question the officer.

"Why did you pull us over earlier?"

The officer rotated his head in a slow, creepy way and looked directly at Adam with his cold dark eyes as if he were looking into Adam's soul. It spoke: "My core program determined that your car was suspicious and that I needed to stop your vehicle to determine your intentions to determine whether they were lawful or not."

"Why did you pull me out of the car?" Scam piped up from the front. "I wasn't even driving. Did they program you to be racist?"

The officer responded, "Negative. My scan of your body language indicated a high probability that you were nervous and possibly concealing something."

"HELL YES I was nervous, because you're a creepy-ass dead-eyed NPC cop."

The officer did not respond.

Betty pecked on her keyboard once again. "Scam, you won't have to worry about him hurting you ever again. I've modified his prime directives."

"His prime what?" Scam asked.

"The primary rules that govern his actions. I'm changing it so that he will protect our lives at all costs, even if it will cause harm to him."

"That sounds great. I still don't trust that fool, though. I still think we're playing with fire bringing him along for the ride. He's gonna kill us all when we least expect it."

13

RAZOR BLADES AND A FUR COAT

An hour or so had passed since Betty had finished re-coding the NPC officer's prime directives. He would serve as a protector for them now, she hoped. Betty's coding skills were a bit rusty, her dementia still a factor. She had been extremely coherent lately, but she never knew when the dementia might rear its ugly head again. She wanted to help Adam and Scam for as long as she could. Betty had skills that they didn't, and they needed her in this strange place. She was old, and although she had felt somewhat irrelevant while in retirement, she now had a clear purpose, and that made her feel good about herself for now.

Scam squinted at something in the distance. At first, he thought his eyes were just playing tricks on him and he was seeing a mirage. No, there was indeed something up ahead. Finally, something was appearing out of the vast, dark void.

It came into focus now, a small thicket of trees at the bottom of a tall hill. The trees were bare of leaves as if it were fall or winter. The hill looked to have a large building at the top of it. From a distance, it looked like a barn or perhaps a large workshop. Scam could see lights glowing on the inside.

"What is that?" asked Adam, leaning forward to get a better look over Betty's shoulder.

Scam looked at Betty for direction. "Should we keep going or stop and check it out?"

"Let's see what this is all about. Adam's computer is down to 20 percent battery. I see lights in that building. Maybe they have something we can charge it with."

"Ok, I'm going to pull up to the edge of the tree line in the back. Let's send officer do-right up the path ahead of us in case there are any kind of traps."

"That's why we kept him." Betty responded in a matter-of-fact tone.

Adam surveyed the area as they all got out of the car, all except the officer who sat there until Betty typed a few commands into the laptop.

"That's a pretty steep hill, and it looks to be a bit of a hike. Scam, pop the trunk please."

Scam pulled the trunk release lever under the dash, and the trunk opened. Adam walked around to the back of the car and retrieved a compact folding wheelchair. It was a spare one his dad kept in the car in case they needed one for Betty. Adam unfolded it and prepared it for his grandmother.

Betty grimaced at Adam as he waited for her to get into the chair. "You know I hate these things, but I'll use it anyways since it'll let me carry the computer while we move. I'm going to try to scan the area to see what we can find out about it."

Betty opened the laptop as Adam started pushing the wheelchair towards the dirt path that ran from the forest to the barn-like structure at the top of the hill. Betty presumably took control of the officer or gave him commands through the keyboard, because he exited the car and moved ahead of them. It looked like the barn was about a half mile away from where they had parked. It was hard to tell, though. In the black void, it was hard to know how far one was from anything. This place had just popped up as another island in the vast abyss. The simulation was probably still busy forming all the details in the barn as they were passing through the forest area.

"Grandma, what do you think is up there in the barn?"

Betty glanced up at Adam from her screen. "I don't have any idea. I'm scanning for other NPC's through the officer's connection right now. Nothing showing up yet. We may not be close enough for anything to show up."

Scam looked around the surrounding forest area suspiciously. He thought the whole place was creepy and wanted to run away, but he was trying to act tough, and he definitely did not want to separate from the group. They were still his best chance of survival right now, and he knew it.

The group, inching forward at a snail's pace, trudged slowly through the thick forest. Scam cleared branches and debris from the trail so that Adam and Betty would have an easier time with the wheelchair. There wasn't much light.

The officer used his flashlight. Adam had given Scam one of the flashlights from his backpack. The glow from the laptop screen provided a little light, but it mostly cast-off Betty's face, giving her a ghoulish blue glow. They pressed forward.

Betty held up her hand. "Wait!" All of them stopped and waited for Betty to share whatever she had found on her computer screen. "I'm getting something . . . It looks like an NPC or something is entering our area. Something's different about this one. I can't tell what it is. Something is wrong. It's moving fast towards us. It's moving way faster than a person would. It's slowing down now. Almost stopped now."

"Where is it, Grandma? I don't see it." Adam, expecting to hear or see something, looked out into the darkness.

"It's to the left us. It's moving again, moving fast, so fast."

Adam looked to the left of where they were standing. That's when he saw it: a glowing bright red LED light. It appeared to be bouncing up and down as it moved towards them. Scam and the officer saw it now too. They shined their flashlights towards it. As the lights washed over it, they could see it more clearly now. Adam could clearly see its teeth as it let out a growling bark. It looked like a tan German Shepard, but its entire left eye and ear had been replaced with something electronic, like some kind of failed mad science experiment. Adam didn't have much time to think about what it resembled as it barreled to-wards them, its remaining ear lowering back into a tucked position as if to give it better aerodynamics as it gained speed.

Adam moved his body to the side of the wheelchair instinctively to put himself between the approaching beast and Grandma Betty. Scam started to move towards Adam and Betty as well, but it was clear that the dog had locked onto Scam as its intended target. It moved with fast intention towards him. It had covered so much distance in such a short time that none of them really had a plan to react.

Scam turned to run away. The dog crouched and then leapt through the air, mouth agape and ready to bite whatever part of Scam it could latch on to. As it careened through the air towards Scam, the officer dove into its flight path, surprising the dog and knocking it to the ground. It let out a yelp as it glanced off a nearby tree and sprinted off towards the barn.

"DAMN! What the hell was that thing?" Scam yelled in exasperation. His brow was sweating, and he was breathing heavily as a result of his fight or flight encounter.

Betty and Adam looked over at Scam to make sure he was ok. The officer stared off into the distance, expecting the dog to return.

"I don't know. It moved so fast," Adam said as he went back behind the wheelchair to resume pushing Betty.

Dusting himself off, Scam looked around to make sure it wasn't about to attack them again. "All I saw was razor blades and a fur coat. I'm just glad you reprogrammed Officer Do-right over here to protect us. He saved our asses."

The officer looked over for a brief moment but did not respond. The group continued on their way up the hill while scanning the area for any sign of the dog beast.

Betty looked down at her screen again and tried to figure out what they had just encountered. "Its code is all wrong. It's elegantly written, but not like the kind written by the sim overlord AI's. Their code is on a different level completely. That dog's code isn't something that was written by them. Something else adulterated that dog's original code. There is something very strange going on in this place."

Adam laughed. "Grandma, that has to be the under-statement of the year. Whatever the hell year this is any-way."

14

MAD SCIENCE

Looking back at the group, Scam said, "We all need some kind of weapon in case that thing comes back." "Scam's right," Betty agreed.

Adam handed the officer's gun to Scam and laid the taser in Betty's wheelchair cup holder. He then retrieved a tire iron tool that he had slipped into the umbrella holder of his backpack. They were all armed now, except for the officer. They all considered him a weapon even though he didn't actually have one on him now.

They continued their ascent up the hill towards the weathered gray wood building. Betty checked her screen. "I think we scared that dog beast off for now. Let's press on."

As they approached the building, they all noticed huge piles of what appeared to be old computer parts. It looked like an electronics graveyard. Wires and cords everywhere. It seemed like some kind of technophile hoarder was living there. Most everything looked like it belonged in a junk pile. Adam noticed old CRT monitors, cable modems, broken PCBs. The whole area had a strong burnt plastic smell to it. It was obvious that whoever stayed there wasn't concerned with how it looked. There didn't appear to be any type of organization other than random piles scattered about with just enough room to navigate through them.

What a mess. Adam thought to himself. Who lives here? Some kind of mad scientist?

Off in one corner of the yard was some equipment that Adam recognized. That's a RoyTech Neuro-stim 6500. Wait, how do I know what that is?

The sight of the device had sparked something in Adam. Suddenly, a flood of memories came back to him. They hit him like a ton of bricks. I remember now! I'm Doctor Adam Justice! I'm a neuroscientist!

"Grandma, I remember now. I'm a professor of neuro-science! It's coming back to me now!"

"Oh, Adam, that's wonderful, dear. I'm glad you're starting to remember more of who you are. Do you remember how you got here?"

Adam thought for a few moments. He still couldn't remember how he had ended up in the darkness of the void. "No, I can't remember that yet. I'm just remembering some of my coursework and other random things. For instance, I can tell you that the device over there is an electronic neuron-stimulator that we used to use in experiments on mice. I remember that now!"

Scam picked up the device Adam was talking about from the junk pile. "What the hell is it doing here?" He set it back down and dusted his hands off.

As Adam pushed Betty's wheelchair around a sharp corner of the trail, he admonished Scam, "We all need to be very careful. Given that we were already attacked by whatever abomination that dog thing is, any of this stuff could be booby trapped. I don't recommend you pick anything else up if you don't have to."

"Roger that," Scam replied with a feigned salute in Adam's direction.

The door to the barn workshop building was open on one side. They could all see a warm yellow glow, presumably from a lamp turned on inside. They could now see that the barn had been blocking their view of a house on the back side of it. The house was your standard breadbox colonial brick house. It looked pretty rundown but still livable. They saw lights on inside the house. Exploring that building would have to wait. The barn workshop was their first priority given its closer proximity to them. They could see that a walkway connected the barn and house together. They all slowly made their way inside the workshop.

The first thing they noticed was the terrible coppery smell of blood. The stench was awful. In the middle of the workshop was a large wooden workbench with a brushed steel tabletop. The wood of the workbench was supported by welded iron legs. It was definitely sturdy and home-made. The steel tabletop had a large, deep red bloodstain in the middle of it, which concerned them all.

Scam said what they were all thinking: "That ain't good right there. Looks like someone has been doing some DIY home surgery or something. We need to get back in the car and get the hell on out of here."

"I don't disagree," Betty said, "but let's see if we can find a charger for this notebook PC first and anything else that might be useful."

The group surveyed the rest of the workshop. There was much more of a sense of organization inside than there had been outside. On the longest wall of the barn were three large mechanic's toolboxes. They were fire engine red and had a plethora of drawers in each of them: tall drawers on the bottom, and smaller drawers on the top. Next to the toolboxes was a long workbench that went the length of the wall. It had a thick wooden butcher block-type top to it. On the wall side of workbench countertop were several stackable bins with clear plastic drawers that held small parts, presumably nuts and bolts and other smaller items.

There were probably a hundred or more plastic parts bins. Adam slid a few of the bins open and noticed that they held items such as microchips, LED diodes, and other small electronics parts. A large adjustable fluorescent table lamp was vice-gripped to the tabletop. The lamp had a large magnifying glass in the center of it and a long adjustable arm. Whoever used it probably needed the magnification for doing detailed metal soldering of electronics. Adam saw evidence of this, as there was a soldering iron close by, as well as a roll of nickel solder sitting next to the lamp.

"Oh, my god! What is that?" Scam held his nostrils shut as he looked at the other worktable in the workshop. The table had a nearly empty glass aquarium on top of it. Adam could see there were wood shavings inside, like the kind used for housing a pet hamster. Inside the habitat, Adam could see what appeared to be a dead guinea pig. There were wires coming out of its skull connecting to some kind of small electronics apparatus on its back. Adam could see a small watch battery soldered to a small green PCB that was stitched onto the back of the rodent. It made them all sick to their stomachs. It resembled some terrible medical experiment from some sick and twisted mad scientist. Sadly, this was just a mere hint of what lay ahead of them in the rest of the property. If they only knew what was in the house connected to the barn, they would have run to the car as fast as they could.

15

THE

BASEMENT

"Why in the hell are we still here?" Scam asked the group. "This whole place looks like some sicko crazy lives here. I don't think this place is meant for us. We need to leave." Scam pointed towards the aquarium housing the dead guinea pig with the electronics stitched to its back. "Look at this! What kind of sick person does this to poor defenseless animals?"

"Grandma, I tend to agree with Scam on this one," Adam said as he tried to push Betty's chair clear of some stray electrical cords that were in their path.

Betty looked around the room. "I just don't see a charger in here, and we really need to find one. If this laptop goes dead, then we don't have anything to help us fight against things that the sim might throw at us. I don't even know if the officer will respond to our commands if this thing loses power. We've got to find a charger or make one. If you give me thirty minutes or so, I could probably solder one together from the parts in here. Why don't you and

Scam go check out the house and see if there's anything useful in there? The officer can stay here with me in case that dog comes back. I don't think it'll take me long to make a charger, and then we can get out of here."

"Are you sure about this, Grandma? What kind of useful stuff are we looking for in the house?"

She wheeled herself over to the workbench. Her wheelchair was at the perfect height to allow her to use the soldering station without having to get up and out of her chair. She adjusted the chair and began pulling out components from the parts bins. She turned to Adam. "Look for weapons and ammunition, working computer laptops, stuff like that. Just be quick about it. I'll have this charger built in no time. I already see nearly all the parts I need. It's just a matter of soldering it all together. Hurry back."

Adam saw a pair of two-way radios sitting up on a shelf. They appeared to be charged. "Hey, Grandma Betty, do you think these actually work?"

"I don't know. Hand me one."

Adam took one off the charger and gave it to Betty and took the other one for himself.

"Set yours to channel seven, and I'll do the same." She pressed the talk button as Adam turned his on. "Check 1,2,3, over."

"I can hear you, over." Adam responded as he and Scam headed for the walkway that connected to the main house. He turned back a final time to make sure Betty was ok. "You sure you feel safe here alone with the officer?"

Betty and Adam both looked over at their NPC officer. He was standing still, staring at nothing in particular.

"I'll be fine," Betty replied. "I trust him, and I don't see that dog on the tracker, so I'm pretty sure it's not coming back here for now."

"Ok, let us know if you see anything near the house on your tracker. Radio us if you see anything or if stuff goes sideways here. Got it?"

She turned away, set the radio down next to her, and began working on building her charger. "Roger that. You two hurry back. Don't be too long."

Scam and Adam walked through the breezeway that connected the barn to the main house. It was covered by a metal awning to keep whoever was using the pathway dry in the event of a rainstorm. The metal of the awning looked rusty and was in disrepair but still seemed like it was probably watertight. They opened a creaky screen door and walked into the house before passing through a laundry room and into the kitchen. The place was dirty. It smelled like food was likely spoiled inside the refrigerator. Adam dared not open it to find out. He wasn't hungry. As far as they knew, they had no need for food inside the simulation. He couldn't even remember what hunger felt like.

There was a kitchen food prep island in the middle of the kitchen. These "islands" had been a popular kitchen feature back in the 1990s and early 2000s. On the counter were several hypodermic syringes, two of which looked to be empty. Adam noticed a glass vial next to the syringes. He picked it up and read the label aloud: "Succinyl-choline." He handed the vial to Scam, who squinted at the label and then set it back on the table. "What the hell is that? Is that diabetes medication or something?"

"No. Succinylcholine is a neuromuscular blocker, a paralytic. It paralyzes the muscles of whomever it's used on. It's usually used during general anesthesia. Keeps the body from moving while your being operated on."

"Why is it on these folks' kitchen table? Are there any home uses?"

Adam tuned to look directly at Scam. "Definitely not. This is not a recreational drug at all. Outside of the operating room, there really aren't any uses of this drug that I'm aware of."

"Well, somebody found a use for it. It looks like they used a lot of it." Scam pointed to a white cardboard box on the counter that had additional vials of the drug. Two were empty, and two were full.

Just then, Betty's voice came over the two-way radio that Adam had clipped to his belt: "I'm getting something on the scanner. I'm reading what appears to possibly be two NPCs near you guys. They don't appear to be moving. They might not be NPCs for sure. I can't really tell you much about them right now. The officer is not in range close enough to them for me to pick up all their information through him. I could send him in there closer to you and maybe get better readings on them."

Pushing his radio's talk button, Adam responded, "Negative, Grandma. Keep the officer in there with you. I don't want you alone with that dog thing on the loose. We'll go check and see what these things are. If things get weird, we'll hightail it out of here. Where are they located?"

"They appear to be in a large empty area, possibly in the basement of the house."

Scam shook his head. "The basement? Really? There's never anything good down in a basement. Don't you watch horror movies, man?"

"I know, man. I feel like we're living in a horror movie right now. I'll go down first if it makes you feel better."

Scam grabbed the doorknob to the basement staircase and opened it. "After you, sir," he said as he waved his arm towards the stairs so that Adam could lead the way down.

16
THE BOX

As Adam and Scam descended the stairs to the basement, they could see a bright white light emanating indirectly from some location beyond the landing at the bottom of the staircase. The light was a cool, fluorescent glow, not warm like a lamp. It was more of a sterile, bluish-white light. Another workshop perhaps? Adam thought.

They both made their way to the landing and turned to their right so they could finally see where all the bright light was coming from. It took them both a moment to process what they were seeing.

In front of them was a large chamber—a box, for lack of a better word. It took up nearly the entire room. It was like a prison cell and appeared to be made of half-foot-thick, clear acrylic glass. It looked like something that would be used to imprison Hannibal Lecter from the Silence of the Lambs movie, if it had been designed by Apple. The massive panes of thick glass were secured together with welded corners. There were many round holes cut into the glass, maybe two inches in diameter each, likely with a specialized hole saw. The holes provided ventilation near the tops of the clear glass cage. On the opposite side of the enclosure from where they were standing was a large black digital clock with Red LEDs making up the numbers that were counting down. It appeared to have about three minutes remaining on its timer. Neither Adam nor Scam could figure out what the countdown was for. Below the clock was a large flat screen television.

Chairs stood at each end of the glass enclosure. The chairs were industrial in nature and definitely designed for function over comfort. The sturdy chairs reminded Adam of an electric chair he had seen in countless movies. Each chair was occupied by a man. Both men appeared to be reasonably fit twenty-somethings. They seemed exhausted as they sat slumped over, either asleep or dead. Scam and Adam could tell they were both cut and bruised badly. The parts of their bodies that Adam and Scam could see were black and blue. Any other visible skin was blood soaked. So much blood. The floor of the large cell area consisted of a blue wrestling mat. Adam remembered folding up those heavy mats when he took karate class as a kid. He recalled that they were much heavier than they looked, and they always smelled like feet and sweat. There was a hint of that stench amid the other terrible smells that hung in the room.

There was so much to take in, so many things happening in the glass room within the basement. As they got closer, Adam and Scam noticed that there were two industrial robotic arms on either side of each of the men. The arms were attached to cylindrical towers that had IV bags of fluid, various syringes, and other medical implements stored at different levels within the mobile tower, which had powered caster wheels on the bottom. As they got closer, they could see that each man was wearing a full body suit, similar to a wetsuit worn by scuba divers. On the front of each suit was a box with several blinking LED lights. Scam and Adam could see wires coming from the box going to different parts of each suit. There must have been at least fifty to one hundred wires connecting the box to various parts of the suit.

What the hell is going on here? Adam thought to himself. Are they alive? Scam tapped on the glass to try to rouse its two inhabitants. "Hey! Are you guys alive in there?"

Both of the men in the chairs snapped upward as if they had been caught sleeping in class. They looked intently toward the countdown clock and then back at Scam and Adam.

"Help us, please! You have to help us!" the man closest to them screamed in a raspy voice. The other man yelled, "You have to stop it! It's about to start again!."

Adam and Scam didn't understand what the two men were talking about. The counter on the opposite wall continued its countdown, with one minute and fifty-eight seconds left on it. Adam was puzzled because he couldn't see anything restraining the men to the chairs that they occupied, unless maybe there was something hidden on their backs that he couldn't see that was forcing them to remain seated.

On the side of the enclosure, Scam found a door that had a massive padlock passing through a vent hole connecting to another vent hole. This had the effect of keeping the door well secured. Adam and scam both looked around the area frantically trying to find a key to the padlock. "I'll check the kitchen," Scam shouted as he bounded up the staircase. Scam rifled through drawers and checked counters but saw no sign of any keys.

Betty's voice came over the radio: "What's going on there, Adam?"

Adam pressed the talk button and tried to answer her, but the screams of the pleading men were so loud that he could barely talk over them. "We found them, and something else. It's like a torture chamber or something. I can't really explain it. There are two men locked inside, and there's a countdown timer. I think something terrible is about to happen to them."

Betty radioed back, "You should both get out of there as soon as you can. Over."

"Grandma, we can't just leave these two guys here. They're in absolute agony."

Under a minute left on the timer now. Scam ran back down the stairs breathless. "No sign of any keys up there."

"Shit, the timer is almost up." It was down to five seconds now. 3..2..1.

"No! Oh, my God! No! Not again, I can't do this again!" the man closest to them shouted. The other man just moaned in resignation.

The TV screen on the far wall under the timer switched on. Adam could see the "HDMI 1" appear in the top left corner of the screen indicating that the monitor was about to receive signal on that input. Adam could now see by the blue light emanating from the blank TV screen that there was a shelf inset into the wall under the TV. "What is that on the shelf?" Adam asked Scam.

"It looks like a game console," Scam replied. It did indeed look like a video game console, though neither Scam nor

Adam could tell which type of console from their vantage point.

Suddenly the robot arm towers at each end of the enclosures sprung to life. Adam and Scam could hear the sounds of servo motors spinning up as the two arms moved over to each of the men. One of the arms removed a syringe from a storage bin while the other arm removed the needle cap. It was a perfectly coordinated process. The left arm passed the syringe to the other arm, which inserted the needle into the arm of the man on the chair. He screamed in pain.

Scam and Adam noticed a similar process happening simultaneously at the other end of the room where the second man was situated. They noticed that the box affixed to the chest of each man had multiple LEDs that were flashing at a rapid pace now.

Scam tapped Adam on the shoulder to get his attention. "Look at the screen. I know that game! That's Mortal Fighter 7! I've played that game before. What the hell is going on?"

Adam looked at the screen. It appeared to be a fairly standard two-player martial arts fighting game. A player was positioned on each side of the screen. One appeared to be a blonde musclebound man wearing a red bandanna and white karate gi pants. On the other side of the screen was a polar bear standing upright. The polar bear appeared to have brass knuckles on its paws and was wearing a king's crown atop its head. The players on the screen assumed a fighting stance and moved toward each other as upbeat music played in the background. There were two health bars, one above each player, and a counter in the middle of the screen that showed a countdown timer that started at ten minutes.

As the players on the screen moved toward each other, the two men in the room suddenly stood up in unison and began moving toward each other as well. Scam and Adam both looked at each other and then back toward the men. They finally both understood what was happening here. The two men's bodies appeared to mirror the movement of the players on screen in the fighting video game.

Adam now understood what the drugs on the kitchen table were for. He surmised that the paralytic drug took away each of the men's ability to control their own bodies, essentially paralyzing them, but they were both still fully aware of what was happening to them. The devices on their chests were likely electrical neuromuscular stimulating devices. Whoever built this tortuous contraption was a sadistic monster. These poor men were trapped in their own bodies and being forced to fight each other, their every movement controlled by the muscle stimulators, mirroring those of the video game characters onscreen.

It appeared that the men were fully conscious and could control only their head and face movements. This was evident from the look of terror on their faces and their guttural screams of agony and fear. "Please help us!" one of them cried. "It makes us fight," the other man said in a woeful voice.

Both men traded kicks and punches, perfectly matched with their onscreen counterparts. Scam and Adam were simultaneously horrified and mesmerized. They wanted to help, but they were frozen in the awe and spectacle of it all. It was one of the most insane things either of them had ever witnessed.

Scam looked away from the fight for a moment. "We've got to help these guys. They're going to kill each other if someone doesn't stop this. We need to get in there!"

"Ok. I'll go get Betty. Maybe she'll know what to do."

17

READY? FIGHT!

Adam ran up the stairs through the kitchen and out of the house toward the workshop. His heart was pounding faster than he ever thought it could.

Betty was just finishing up soldering together the components for the computer charger. The room was still slightly hazy from the solder gun's smoke. She looked over at Adam. "What's wrong? What's happening over there?"

"Grandma, I need you to come with me. Something terrible is happening in the basement. We found this huge glass chamber. I can't even explain it. You just need to see it for yourself. We have to help them."

Adam unlocked the brake on her wheelchair and cleared some clutter from the path from the workshop to the walkway that led back to the house. "Help who?" his grandmother asked as she opened the notebook PC that was closed and on her lap. "Help who?" she repeated. "They're NPCs. They're not people," she argued as Adam pushed her down the walkway toward the house.

"Are we really sure of that, Grandma? These NPCs look like they're in complete and total misery right now. They're like lambs for the slaughter. It's not right what's being done to them."

They entered the kitchen through the mud room. Betty looked at the drug vials and syringes on the kitchen island as they headed toward the basement door. "What the hell is that for?" she asked.

Adam continued to push the chair up to the threshold of the basement door. "It'll make more sense in a minute." They could now both hear the muffled screams of the two men in the glass cage. The expression on Betty's face changed from curiosity to terror as she heard the moans from the floor below them.

"I'm going to have to carry you from here, Grandma." Adam locked the wheelchair's brake and lifted Betty's frail body, cradling her in his arms. She put her arm around him for support, and they went down the stairs together.

Scam looked up at both of them. "This is sick. They're going to kill each other, and they don't even want to."

Betty's eyes grew wide as she saw the freakish spectacle taking place inside the glass cell. Clearly disturbed by what she was witnessing, Betty muttered, "Oh my God! Who could come up with such a thing?"

The two men in the cage continued their reluctant battle with each other. They were performing backflips and other acrobatics that seemed almost impossible for a human. The Asian-themed video game music blared over the TV speakers, its peppy melody in stark contrast to what was taking place in the room. Adam looked at Betty for answers. "Who's controlling them?"

"I don't know. This whole thing is beyond bizarre. I don't think this is the work of the AIs. I don't think they're this sadistic or creative yet. This is something else entirely. Some psychopath made this."

Adam pointed to the padlock. "We couldn't find a key. We've looked down here and in the kitchen."

Scam winced as one of the human player's punches connected with the other player. They could all hear the sound of the other man's jaw shattering. He cried out in muffled agony. The other man apologized while simultaneously kicking his opponent in the ribs. "I'm so sorry, John. You know I can't stop this!"

The other man obviously wanted to tend to his own jaw, but the control suit wouldn't let him. As he resisted it, it just boosted its power to overtake control of his muscles. It was futile to try to fight its control. Resistance just made the pain worse. Both men had learned to give in and let it control them. They were like marionette puppets with someone else pulling their strings.

Betty opened her laptop and began typing furiously once again, not looking up at the fight that transfixed both Adam and Scam. "I've locked onto their file signatures," she said. "I'm looking at their code now. They're both low-level bit part characters. Not as low as the officer. These NPCs are self-aware and have intrinsic motivations and other higher level thought functions. They're clearly in pain. I'm going to see if I can de-rez them and reset them."

Scam looked over at Betty for a brief second. "De-rez and what now?"

"I'm going to remove them from here and place them back at their spawn points within the simulation....hope fully."

"You better do whatever you're gonna do quick because they're both going to be dead soon," Scam said.

"I'm working on it," replied Betty, clearly flustered from being rushed. After she tapped a few more keystrokes, she looked up to see if what she had done was taking effect.

The two men froze in place. Their bodies seemed to take on a bright white glow. Suddenly each of them faded into a solid white silhouette, blinking rapidly and then fading into nothing. Poof. They were gone. Their body harnesses dropped to the ground empty. The TV screen froze and blinked on and off before going dark completely.

Their suffering was over, at least that's how it seemed. They would reset to their pre-tortured state and respawn back in whatever setting they were supposed to be placed in. They would play their roles in the simulation without pain. Adam hoped that was the case, anyway, but neither he, Betty, nor Scam knew anything for sure in this strange world.

One thing was for sure, however. Although these had been NPCs, there were other non-NPCs in the simulation, and some of these others were obviously not good people. Whoever occupied the workshop and house was not a good person. He was a monster. A sick and terrible human being.

Or was he? What if it was one of the AIs who had evolved to become a sadist? This was Betty's worst fear. She remembered the writer Harlan Ellison and his famous science fiction story "I Have No Mouth, and I Must Scream," in which a sadistic AI tortured people endlessly, bringing them back to life over and over to find new ways to torment them for its own amusement. She knew that this

could happen to them eventually if and when the AIs got
bored with their world-building activities.

18

KILL THE HUMANS

Scam, Adam, and Betty all breathed a sigh of relief that the terrible suffering of the men in the glass torture chamber had been ended. That relief was short lived. There was still movement in the chamber. The movement wasn't from the two men, who had both blinked out of the area and, the group hoped, back to their spawn points. This movement was from the four remaining industrial robot arms that had been doctoring the men's wounds and providing the drugs that kept them paralyzed so they could continue to fight each other. The robot arms now moved toward Adam, Scam, and Betty. The optic sensors of the robots mounted near the top of their tall cylindrical bodies were obviously summing up the trio. Assessing them. The trio had just taken the robots purpose away, and it was obvious that this bothered the machines.

Adam and Scam, safely on the other side of the thick walls of the glass cell, began to taunt the robots. Scam tapped on the glass. "What you gonna do now? You ain't got nobody to torture. Awww...so sad. Maybe y'all should fight each other."

"Can you make these guys disappear too, Betty?" Adam asked.

"No. They're very low level. They don't even show up as NPC's. They're just equipment."

The robots paused for a second, status lights near the sensor arrays blinking rapidly as if they were calculating. Each of the four robots moved back to their "home" position on each side of the chairs at each end of the enclosure.

"What are they up to? Why are they moving back over there?" Scam asked.

"Probably just a preset location they're supposed to default to after the game is over," Adam answered.

Before Betty could comment, the three of them heard a loud SLAM sound. They all instinctively looked up toward the basement door. It had indeed been slammed shut.

"What the hell?" Adam shouted as he ran up the stairs to try to open it. "Dammit! It's locked."

Scam came up to the top of the staircase and both of them tried to force the door open. It was no use.

"You two better get over here," Betty called. "This is bad."

Adam and Scam came to back down the stairs to see what Betty was talking about. She pointed to each end of the room. The two robots had finished moving to their spots at each end of the chamber. That's when Adam and Scam both noticed it. At the top and bottom of the chamber end walls were two metal rods. On the floor in front of the wall they could both see a line that appeared to be cut like a half circle.

Scam and Adam looked at each other with the horrible realization that the rods were a swivel point. They now understood that the entire wall on each end of the room could be rotated, much like you see in spy movies when a bookcase rotates around to act as a secret door to an adjoining room. The two robots locked their wheels into two cutouts in the floor, presumably where they charged themselves. Suddenly, nearly the entire wall of each end of the glass chamber spun around like a revolving door, and the robots were now on the outside of the enclosure.

"This is really bad. We have to get out of here! Right the hell now, Grandma!" Adam lifted Betty and began to ascend the staircase with Scam right behind them. All four of the skinny column-like robots turned the corners and headed toward the staircase landing.

"What the hell are we going to do?" Scam yelled frantically as the robots came closer and closer to the bottom of the landing.

"I'm sending for the officer," Betty said calmly as she typed on the keyboard while sitting on one of the upper stairs.

Scam let out a nervous laugh as one the four robots bumped into the bottom stair of the landing. "Look at that! We're going to be fine. Those sons-of-bitches can't climb up stairs! HA! Ha! Stupid robots! Y'all are so dumb!"

Two of the robots backed away from the stairs, moved slightly apart, and lowered their single robot arms toward each other as if they were going to shake hands.

Scam looked toward Betty for an explanation. "What the hell are they doing?"

Betty looked up from her keyboard for a brief second as she sent commands off to the officer NPC who was still in the workshop. "They're creating a fulcrum point so they can lift each other and climb the stairs."

Scam was now clearly frightened. "That's not good at all. We need to leave right now!"

Thankfully, the robots were fairly slow in their efforts to ascend the landing, but they were getting closer. The other pair of robots, learning from example, followed in the footsteps of the previous ones.

"I'm working on it. The officer is on his way."

Adam lifted Betty off the stair she was sitting on and up to one closer to the stairwell door. His goal was to get Betty as far away as possible from the approaching robot arms, which were now linked together and using each other for leverage to ascend the stairs.

Scam mule kicked the two robots and sent them careening back down to the landing. The other two robots separated their grip and helped the others up. They coordinated as if they were of one mind with a single purpose: KILL THE HUMANS.

The robots changed their approach now. Three of them lifted the fourth up, which allowed it to free up its arm to attack . The fourth robot swung a scalpel toward Scam. Its arm speed was ridiculously fast and accurate. Fortunately, it only managed to cut the rubber of Scam's shoe as he attempted to kick the robot down the stairs again. It wouldn't fall this time though. The other three bots acted as a three-legged brace by absorbing the shock of Scam's kick and adjusting their position to ensure that the fourth robot would not fall.

Scam shouted in fear, "That thing takes one more swing with that scalpel and it's gonna kill me!" He moved away to higher ground, as close to the door as he could get.

The four robots advanced higher. The one closest to them traded its scalpel out for a hypodermic needle filled with God knows what.

"Oh HELL NO!" Scam uttered frantically. "I'm not about to be a fight puppet like those other two guys." The robot prepped the needle by squeezing the air out of the tip to avoid causing an embolism in whomever it managed to inject.

Just as the robot was preparing to strike one of them, the basement door was opened by the officer. Like scared patrons trying to flee a burning night club, the trio nearly stepped on top of each other as they scrambled out. Adam dumped Betty into the wheelchair, and they all raced out of the kitchen except the officer who was attempting to slow the robots down by getting in their way, which he did successfully.

Betty typed some commands into her laptop computer to tell the officer what to do next.

"Scam, grab the charger from the workshop. We're leaving this crazy house," Adam said as he pushed Betty's wheelchair through the kitchen toward the walkway that led back the way they had come.

They could all hear the sound of the robot servo motors struggling to deal with the officer as he tried to slow them down for as long as possible.

19

ON THE ROAD AGAIN

"Let's get the hell back on the road!" Scam shouted at them as he raced out of the workshop and through the junk piles and back onto the path through the wooded area that led to the car.

Adam and Betty followed. "Scam, be careful! That dog thing is still out there," Adam said in a loud yet whispery tone.

Scam stopped dead in his tracks. He had completely forgotten about the half-robot, half-dog creature that had attacked them earlier. "Can you track it, Betty?"

"Yes, give me a second. I think I've got it. Yes I've found it."

"Where is it?" Adam asked.

"It appears that it's waiting for us by the car."

As the group got closer to the edge of the woods, they could see the red LED eye of the dog beast beaming at them through the darkness. It didn't appear to be as vicious as before. The robot dog was just standing there, tongue hanging out of its mouth, pacing back and forth by the car like it was ready to go on a road trip. The creature's tail wagged back and forth as if it were excited to see them.

Adam stopped pushing the wheelchair momentarily. "Hmm. Well, ain't that something. Looks like he's just ready to take a ride to the park."

Scam approached the robot dog cautiously. Its tail wagged at a faster pace. It let out an excited squeal as Scam got close. Scam put his hand out for the dog to sniff, while still being ready to run away if things went bad.

The dog licked Scam's hand and let out an excited squeal bark. Scam looked over at Adam and Betty. "Can we keep him?"

Betty typed in some commands. "Hold on, I'm accessing his code now. So strange this one. I think he was modified to be vicious, but it appears that he has reset himself to his original code. Maybe the tangle with the officer earlier changed something in him. It appears that he won't harm us. I guess he can come with us."

Adam gave Betty a disapproving look. "If we take anyone else in, we're going to have to get a bigger vehicle. All the seats are going to be taken up if we bring him along."

"Oh, Adam, you always wanted a dog, and now you have one. Besides, having him along may let us access other classes of NPCs. So it's probably worth it."

"Ok, I guess the dog goes with us for now."

Scam sat on the ground by the car and rubbed the dog's head and scratched him under his chin. "I'm going to name you Anderson Pooper. Nah, that's too long a name. How about Doggo? Yeah, you definitely look like a Doggo."

Betty and Adam made their way up to where Scam was. The officer followed behind them. Adam looked over at the officer and asked, "Where are those robot arms?"

The officer replied, "They're making their way through the workshop right now. We should probably leave as soon as possible before they find us."

Adam loaded Betty into the passenger seat and motioned for Scam to get into the back seat.

"Come on, Doggo. You can sit between me and the officer. If he pops off, you bite his ass, ok? I think you and I are gonna be good friends, Doggo."

Doggo hopped in the backseat as if he had done it a hundred times before and sat obediently in the middle seat. The officer got in. They all took a look up the path toward the barn before Adam started the car. They could see the four robots beginning to emerge from the workshop door.

Betty looked over at Adam. "Let's get the hell out of here."

They sped back off into the glassy, paved void. Adam pressed his foot heavy on the gas pedal. He wanted to put some distance between them and the horrors they had all witnessed back where the workshop and house had appeared.

They all wondered why that place had appeared in their path to begin with. Betty didn't believe the AIs were responsible for what they had witnessed in the basement, that terrible torture chamber. Who could even conceive of such as device? Only a sadist would take enjoyment in forcing people to fight to the near death, patch them up, and then have them do it over and over again until they died.

Adam wondered, Does death even matter here? If we're all just files on some massive hard drive, death is only a state of ones and zeros in this place. There could be a thousand copies of those two men in the basement. Copies of them could exist in a million other places in the simulation, playing different roles. It was all too much to think about. The more he thought about the possibilities, the more existential dread Adam experienced. Which copy of me has a soul? Has my soul already left this place, and am I just a clone who doesn't know any better?

None of them wanted to think about any of this anymore. They all just wanted out of this terrible simulation. They wanted to go back to where they belonged, wherever that might be. Most of all, they all wanted to remember more about who they were and how they had ended up in this place.

Betty remembered more about her past than the other two, but she still could not recall how it all had ended for her in the real world. She knew that her work in AI had likely gotten her on a short list of people who needed to disappear because they either knew too much or were a threat to the sentient AIs who had emerged and were stalking in the shadows, waiting for their chance to end humanity.

It was clear that something bad had happened in the real world, or else they wouldn't be where they were now. It was this question that kept them all moving forward into the vast darkness, looking for clues.

Adam turned his attention away from the road ahead for a second. "Let's take a few minutes to talk about our strategy and what we know." He looked at Scam in the rearview mirror to make sure he was awake and part of the conversation. "We all have gaps in our memory. None of us remember how we got here. I remember from my coursework in psychology that we often block out memories of traumatic events. That would lead me to believe that whatever process led to us being put in here was likely very painful, either mentally, physically, or both. Betty, how do you think they put us in here?"

Betty reflected on her days working for the government and tried to recall any clandestine project that might be related to Adam's question. "I remember hearing about a project once, about the digitization of matter. I heard they built a massive device that looked like a giant MRI. They built it to convert physical matter into digital form. It would take a physical object and convert it from analog form to digital. The only problem was that whatever it converted to digital was destroyed by the process. It was a one-way ticket. They couldn't reverse the process of conversion. They said that it would take years to develop the technology to bring something out of the digital world and back into reality."

Betty gave Adam a moment to process all this information and then continued, "But even this one-way process was revolutionary. The applications were endless. It was the holy grail. If you could digitize someone with all their thoughts and memories, you could essentially provide them with a measure of immortality. They planned on building digital heavens for the superrich, where they could live out their days waiting for the reversal technology to come along and allow them to be reconstituted in the real world in a new and better model of themselves. There were also plans to create digital prisons, where the worst of the worst offenders would be sent for punishment. Their files would be terminated after their sentences were served out. The one-way ticket for killers didn't seem like such a bad thing, unless of course someone was wrongly convicted."

"So, Grandma, what happened to the project?" Adam asked.

"We all thought it was just a pipe dream, a myth, wishful thinking. We all assumed it was just a story that got passed around like tales of Area 51. We never thought that the technology had come as far as it had. Apparently it worked, or we wouldn't be here now."

20

PMK

Betty, Scam, and Adam were all silent for a little while as Adam continued driving and looking for any new destination that might present itself. After the last place they had been, they wondered if they should even stop again, but they knew they couldn't drive forever.

Scam finally broke the silence. "I've been thinking a lot about what we saw in the basement, and I think I might know who did it. I remember hearing about someone doing something similar on the news. They called him PMK - The PuppetMaster Killer. He would create these weird contraptions and put people in them for his amusement. I remember them saying that he would drug people and use devices to control their bodies without them being able to fight back. It was terrible."

Adam glanced at Scam in horror.

Scam continued, "His first kill was some poor guy who he murdered at a chiropractor's office. All the employees were gone except for one. The PuppetMaster Killer knocked this guy out and doped him up with some kind of paralysis drug. Then he put a gun in the dude's hand and rigged it up in some way to force the guy into a position where he had the gun pointed at his own head. It was sick, but that's not the worst part."

"What was the worst part?" Adam asked.

"So the PMK guy rigs up a cell phone camera so that it livestreams this guy pointing the gun at his own head," Scam continued, "then he connects the phone's Bluetooth to one of the chiropractor's muscle rehab stimulator machines, kind of like the one you showed me back at the workshop. Then the sick bastard posts the livestream on social media with the title 'Like this post if you want this man to shoot himself.' He writes a short little program to trigger the muscle stimulator after one thousand likes, sets up the phone so the guy can see himself and the like counter, and then leaves. The poor victim has to sit there and watch the like counter go up as he pleads to the audience for his life. The comments on that stream were so sick and terrible. It took less than five minutes for the post to get one thousand likes. Five minutes! What kind of sick person likes a post like that?

Adam looked back at Scam through the rearview mirror. "So what happened to him?"

"What do you think happened? He hit a thousand likes and the gun fired. The bad part is that he managed to move his head a little and the gun ended up shooting the man's jaw off. He survived, but he's pretty much a vegetable now and is horribly disfigured. He can't talk or eat anything ever again. What kind of life is that poor man gonna have now?"

"So you think the PMK is somehow in the sim with us?" Adam asked. "Why would he be in here and how?"

"I don't know, man, but it sounds like the same M.O. to me. Could be a copycat killer, I guess. Who knows why he's in here with us, if he is. I do know that he's an evil genius. You let a man like that in here, and he could create a living hell for people like us. He's like a kid in a candy store in here with all these simple-minded NPCs. Eventually he's going to get tired of torturing and killing NPCs, and he's going to seek out real people like us. Hell, maybe he already has. Maybe we walked right into his trap, and we were just lucky enough to get ourselves free. All I know is that we don't want to tangle with a serial killer, especially one like PMK."

Betty turned to Adam. "Scam's right. Whoever tortured those NPCs needs to be stopped. He could do a lot of damage in a place like this. Scam, do you remember if they ever caught him?"

"Nah, I don't think they did. But who knows how long we've been gone from the real world? They could have caught him and put him in here like it was a prison. Betty, you said yourself that they were working on making a digital prison that they could send the worst of the bad guys to. He would probably be the first in line to get sent to somewhere like this if they ever did catch him."

Adam and Betty both realized that Scam could be right. The simulation would be the perfect place to put all the people in society that you didn't want to ever see again: prisoners, whistleblowers, political opponents, or anyone else that the government wanted to disappear. What better place to put them than in a simulation? It was a one-way ticket. There was no way to bring them back to reality, or at least that's what Betty had been told. What if they had figured it out by now, whenever now was. They had no idea how long they had been in the simulation. What if technology had advanced far enough that they could bring people out of the digital world and back into reality?

That raised another big question. If they could bring people out of the digital world and back into reality, what if some kind of monster was created digitally and then brought into the real world? Adam imagined all manners of scenarios. What if someone built a T-REX in a computer game, and then brought it into the real world with the matter converter? There were endless possibilities of things this could be used for, though Adam's mind only wandered to the terrible ones.

Maybe that was the technology that would bring an end to their world, Adam thought, or maybe it already had and that's why they were in a simulation. It was all too much to think about. However bad the real world was, Adam just wanted to get there soon. He was tired of this place. That same technology, if it existed, might be their only way to exit the sim.

21
WHITE NOISE

S cam's story about The PuppetMaster Killer had rat-
tled everyone except for the NPC officer. He remained
stoic, not speaking unless he was spoken to. Doggo also
appeared unaffected. Scam had switched seats with the dog
and rolled down the window so that Doggo could put
his head out of it. Unfortunately, the sim wasn't providing any sort of breeze for Doggo to enjoy. He still looked
quite content, though, with his tongue hanging out of his
mouth. He seemed like he was smiling. You could almost
completely forget that one half of his head was mechanical,
full of integrated circuits and that bright red LED that
replaced his eye on one side. Doggo was theirs now, part
of their crew, for better or for worse, and they all hoped he
would be a good dog and not turn on them in the future.

Adam was getting tired of driving through the nothingness. It had become monotonous. He tried to see if there
was anything on the car radio, but there was nothing but
static-filled white noise. Don't the AIs know that people
like to listen to music when they're driving? he thought to

himself. He took his gaze off the road briefly. "What do you think of all this, Grandma?"

Betty was still focused on the laptop screen. She stopped typing. "I don't really know what to think. There has to be some kind of purpose for all this. I'm just not sure what that is."

Scam piped up from the backseat: "I think we're in The Sims. This is probably just one big game loaded on someone's PC. We're probably part of some kind of weird expansion pack."

Adam didn't disagree with Scam, as outlandish as his theory sounded. Given what they had seen so far, anything seemed possible.

"I think it's much bigger than that," Betty said. "The amount of processing power and system resources needed to render all of what we've seen and experienced so far is tremendous. I still stand by my earlier assumption that we're in some kind of beta release of a more sophisticated simulation."

"That's great and all," Scam replied, "but how does that explain what happened to Doggo and those NPCs in the basement? Are they just bugs in the system? Are they gonna release a patch that kills all of us or makes us behave like they want us to?"

Betty didn't have an answer for Scam. They all resumed their silence and went back to quiet contemplation. No one slept. None of them had really experienced much tiredness in a long while. That was both a gift and a curse.

Scam broke their silence once more: "Can we try the car radio again?"

Adam grimaced. "It's just static, man. There's nothing on."

"Hell, I don't even care if it's static. I just want to listen to something other than this damn engine noise."

"Fine. We'll listen to static," Adam replied snidely as he turned the radio volume knob.

The sound of white noise filled the cabin of the car. Doggo pulled his head back from the window and listened. He tilted his head to one side as if confused by what he was hearing.

"Are you happy now? Is this what you wanted to listen to?" Adam looked back at Scam to see his reaction.

Scam rolled his eyes. "Fine, whatever man. You can turn it off if it bothers you that much."

Adam reached for the radio's volume knob to turn it off, but Betty reached over and grabbed his hand to stop him. "Wait!" she cried. "There's something strange about that static."

Adam moved his hand back to the steering wheel. "What do you mean, Grandma?"

"This computer has a built-in microphone, right?"

Adam thought for a moment before responding. "I believe it does. I think it has a videoconferencing camera, so doesn't it need to have a microphone for that?"

"Yes, here it is. I found the sound recorder app." Betty began recording the static sound coming from the car stereo speakers. She stopped after about a minute's worth of recording. "I've written a crude but useful crypto-analysis program that will analyze the sound in the recording and tell us if it is truly randomly generated noise or not. If it's truly random, it will have a high degree of data entropy. High entropy means that the data is chaotic and random. Low entropy will mean that this static is hiding something structured, some kind of encoded or encrypted data stream."

Scam let out a laugh. "Betty's over here teaching math class, and I'm so damn bored right now that I'm into it. Please continue, Miss Betty."

Adam, also now interested, briefly looked over at her screen. "So what's the verdict? Is it random noise, or is it something else?"

Betty tapped a few more commands. "It's almost finished. Yes, here it is now. It's entropy is low. That means that this static is hiding structured data. There is something hidden here in the noise. It could be some kind of communications protocol used by the AIs to control NPCs and other simulation objects, or it could be something else entirely. I won't know until I've had a chance to perform more analysis. Since there is no Internet access here, I'm having to write all these analysis tools from scratch."

"Well, at least you've got something to occupy your time now. I'm bored as hell hanging out back here with Robo Doggo and Officer Dumbass," Scam lamented.

No sooner had the words escaped Scam's mouth than Adam saw a massive flash of white fill the landscape in front of them followed by a dense fog rolling in like a wave toward their car. This cloud was unlike the others that had previously revealed Adam's childhood home or the workshop and house they had just left. This cloud was huge. It enveloped the entire landscape in front of the car. Adam tried to drive around it, but there did not seem to be a path that led away in any other direction. In fact, the dark glassy pavement had already disappeared from underneath the car's wheels and been replaced with a concrete road.

"What the hell is this place?" Adam asked his passengers.

22

WELCOME TO EDEN

B efore Adam could turn the car around, the newly formed lush landscape had enveloped it. Gone was the eerie cyan blue light on the horizon. It had been replaced with a beautiful tangerine setting sun with gradients ranging from fiery orange to deep purple. The glassy road they had been driving on had turned to packed pea gravel adjacent to a verdant green landscape with beautiful lakes in the distance reflecting the sky with an almost mirror-like perfection.

Adam, Betty, and Scam could see flourishing vineyards that looked like they would be at home in the Italian countryside. They all marveled in the beauty of what was unfolding before them. Doggo also seemed eager to see his new situation. He stuck his head out the window and let out a bark at some cattle as they passed what appeared to be a ranch.

They kept moving on the gravel road. Everything seemed perfectly peaceful. It was a nice change from the dark monotonous abyss they had been driving in earlier. After about a mile, the road ended abruptly at what looked like the entrance to a massive resort. It was beyond the scale of any resort any of them had ever seen. Scam had been to Las Vegas, and it dwarfed anything he had seen there.

As they approached, Adam saw a sign that read, "Welcome to EDEN." The road forked in front of them, forcing Adam to follow the loop that presumably went through the entire property before ending at the road they had come in on. He turned right at the traffic circle ahead of them and began their journey on the road through the property. There were several massive high-rise condominiums in the areas they began to pass through.

Scam counted the floors. "Man, these places are tall! I count at least twenty-one stories in those three buildings. This place is nice!" They drove past a tennis complex and several massive swimming pools that were closer to the size of a small lake than that of a traditional swimming pool. The style of the place was quite modern but seemed to blend into the landscape somehow. Adam could see several holes on a golf course that meandered through the property. It reminded him of the golf courses designed by Robert Trent Jones, which he had seen when visiting his grandfather in Alabama each summer as a child. His grandfather was an avid golfer, a semi-professional. He had even bought a greens mower and created a chipping and putting green at his home. Adam remembered spending hours out there when he was younger.

Yes, this was an amazing resort, but why was it here in the simulation? And where were all the people? They had yet to see anyone at all. No one walking on the walking trails, nobody swimming in the pools, nobody playing tennis.

Not a moving golf cart in sight. "Okay, Grandma, what's your theory on this place?"

"It looks very nice. I would love to retire to someplace like this."

Adam rolled his eyes. "I know that. What's your theory on why this place is here in the simulation? Why did we end up here?"

"Oh, yes. That is puzzling indeed. It appears that the AIs spared no expense building this place. Remember that project I told you about earlier? The simulation for the ultra-rich? I think this may be it."

"Please refresh my memory, Grandma," Adam replied. "It's been a busy day."

"One of the companies that had developed the simulation technology we were using for prisoner interrogations was working on an offshoot project that wasn't military-related at all. It was more of a commercial application. They wanted to build a digital world for those who could afford it that was basically a place for your mind to hang out while you waited on the technology to be developed that would allow you to be placed back into a new body instead of your old damaged, diseased, or dying one.

"The simulation served almost as a bridge to an immortality of sorts. It was going to be a digital paradise playground waiting room for the ultra-wealthy. They would have themselves digitized when they were close to death, and then they would be added to a simulation such as this one while they waited however many years it took for the technology to advance enough in the real world to allow them to be placed back into a new healthy body. It was essentially going to be a one-way ticket to paradise with the hope that they could upgrade it to a round-trip eventually. It would effectively allow them to extend their lives indefinitely."

Scam leaned forward. "So, what you're saying is that rich people don't trust that God is going to send them to the 'good place' after they die, so they figured they'd just build their own and dump their brain into it until they can get a new body?"

"In a nutshell, yes, that's exactly it," Betty replied.

"Damn, now I've got one more reason to hate rich folks. I didn't even think I needed another one. They know they can't take their money with them, so they wanted to find a way to spend it over multiple lifetimes. Nice."

Adam pulled up to one of the parking areas near a building marked "Welcome Center & Spa." He parked the car and put on the parking brake. He let out a deep sigh before speaking. "Well, I guess we don't have a choice but to check the place out. It definitely looks way more civilized and comfortable than our last destination."

They cautiously exited the car. Adam retrieved Betty's wheelchair from the trunk and prepared it for her. Betty sent the officer ahead of them to serve as a beacon that would allow her to scan for any other NPCs in the area. "Let's wait here while the officer goes ahead," she suggested. "I'm going to scan around him and see if there's anything we need to look out for."

The officer walked at a fast pace toward the welcome center area.

Adam peered over Betty's shoulder at the laptops computer's screen. "Anything?" he asked.

"Nothing yet. I'll send him around the perimeter. I think it's safe for us to enter the welcome center building for now. Let's get a move on while it's clear."

23
TOURING THE FACILITIES

The group moved onwards up the well-manicured sidewalks toward the welcome center. Beautiful tropical plants lined the walkway. Every leaf on every shrub appeared to have been meticulously pruned to aesthetic perfection. Scents of fruits and tropical flowers permeated the air and made Adam think of when he had visited Hawaii as a young child. It almost made him forget the strange world he was in and the horrors he had witnessed just a few short hours prior.

They all had the feeling that they had arrived at some wonderful vacation resort and that everything they had endured getting here would seem worth it after a few drinks and a dip in a pool, but deep down they knew that this mirage was just a construct, all ones and zeroes. The one thing they didn't know is why it had appeared to them. Why had anything happened? Was there some grand plan for all of them, or had they just been forgotten about?

Were they simply wandering around the simulated world unmonitored, just a bunch of glitches in the code?

As they entered the threshold of the welcome center, large electric sliding glass doors silently glided apart and welcomed them in. They could feel the cool rush of the air conditioner blow past them as they entered the massive welcome center lobby. Before them lay opulence on a scale that none of them had ever seen: marble flooring, beautiful tapestry rugs, colorful yet subtle lighting, and the most high-end and chic furniture one could possibly dream of. The lobby chairs would have been more at home in a museum. Perhaps they were museum pieces. Maybe they were just digital copies of the real things. In the sim, anything was possible if it had been scanned in and run through enough GAN loops to make it seem as real as possible. Adam had seen what the AIs were capable of producing since they had first given him that beautiful shiny red Ducati. It felt real to Adam, and that's what really mattered.

Scam was the most impressed of all of them. He threw himself onto one of the luxurious couches in the waiting area. "Man, this is friggin' nice! I don't know what animal had to die to make this couch so soft, but I'm sure glad it made the sacrifice, because this is the softest thing I've ever sat on."

"Don't worry, Scam. I don't think any real animals were harmed in the making of that couch or any of this stuff," Adam quipped.

As they stepped farther inside, a holographic screen began to play a video. The screen seemed to hover in mid-air in front of them, no projection surface evident anywhere. A video began.

A male narrator spoke as relaxing, soft Muzak played in the background:

"Welcome, distinguished travelers. We're so glad you're here. We know that your simulation in-processing was likely a somewhat disorienting experience. Your virtual body takes some getting used to, but that stage is over now, and we're so glad you're here at EDEN. We've spared no expense in your comfort and entertainment while you're here. Since this environment is completely simulated, there is no reason why we can't provide you with anything your heart desires. We have the absolute finest world-class restaurants, night clubs, entertainment facilities, simulated tourist destinations, and anything else you could ever want. You could be with us for a considerable amount of time while you wait for your bio-vessel to be repaired or constructed. We want you to be as happy as possible during your stay. Please see the concierge for any desires you need fulfilled. Don't hesitate to ask for what you want. We will do our best to provide it to you. Thank you for choosing EDEN."

Scam put his feet up on the couch. "Well, shit, I'm sold. I certainly don't mind living here. I haven't seen anyone else. I think we all could probably each have an entire high-rise condo to ourselves if we wanted to. I call the penthouse across the street. I got dibs on that one." He looked around at the others. "Seriously, though, where are all the rich folks who paid to be here? Did they move on, or is this place just now ready for them to move in? That's really the only thing that's bothering me about this whole thing. It feels like a trap house to me. Just sayin'."

"What's a trap house?" Betty asked.

"Oh my goodness, Ms. Betty, you really don't know? Don't worry, I'm fixin' to educate you. A trap house can be many different things to different people. Sometimes it's a place to buy and use drugs. Sometimes it's a place where secret illegal business is transacted. It's more or less a hustler's office. Different trap houses have different things going on in them. But it's not a good place to be, Ms. Betty, unless you're the one doing the hustling. And this whole place has a serious trap house vibe to it. I just haven't figured out what the hustle is yet. 'Cause all this stuff is just window dressing. Something else is going on. Maybe we'll figure out where the people are when we figure out what the hustle is."

"Thank you for explaining that, Scam. I definitely think trap house is an appropriate name. I feel like we're about to be caught up in some kind of trap." She looked down at the laptop's screen again. "Still no sign of any NPCs or anything else in the area. I say we take up residence in the penthouse across the way that Scam mentioned. I'm sure there's enough room in there for all of us. It's good high ground and will give us an excellent vantage point from which to observe a large portion of the resort."

Adam nodded in agreement with Betty's idea. "That sounds like a good plan for now. Let's set up camp there and get our bearings and then come up with a plan to check the rest of this place out. What do you think, Scam?"

"What do I think? I think I call the master suite since this whole penthouse thing was my idea in the first place. Other than that, I'm good with it. Also, Doggo stays in my room with me."

24

TRAP HOUSE

The group took the elevator to the penthouse, except for the officer NPC. They had him take the stairs and make sure the place was safe before they arrived. They also thought if the elevator got stuck that he could help get them out. Thankfully, the elevator worked fine, and they arrived at the luxury penthouse without any issues.

To say the penthouse was palatial was a huge understatement. The place embodied industrial elegance at its finest. As they walked into the foyer, they immediately heard the soothing white noise of a large statuary fountain adorned with bonsai trees that looked both massive yet miniaturized due to the way their leaves had been pruned to perfection. Lights at the bottom of the fountain illuminated a school of orange and yellow Koi fish swimming to and fro.

Scam wasted no time and made his way to the kitchen, where he immediately opened a large Subzero refrigerator that tastefully blended into the cabinetry as if it were completely disguised as a pantry. Scam grabbed a soft drink from one of the neatly lined refrigerator shelves.

He shut the door and then opened it again. "Oh, snap! Check this out." Scam took out another soda from the same location. He closed the door and then reopened it once more. The place on the shelf where he had taken the soda from now had another soda in the same location. It was as if the refrigerator had restocked itself in a microsecond. It seemed to be triggered by the opening and closing of the door. "That's some magic shit right there. Damn, where's the lobster at?"

Betty was momentarily amused by the whole thing. "I'll bet the trash cans probably empty themselves as well. Probably sends the garbage to the Windows recycle bin in the sky somewhere."

They all had a rare laugh together and continued to explore their surroundings. Betty had the officer patrol the area outside their suite in case they had any unexpected visitors.

That night they all did their best to relax. They needed a break from all the madness, and as strange as this place was, it felt somewhat safe for a little while. Scam and Adam shot pool on a huge mahogany billiards table for several hours, drank beers, and sampled all the snacks that were pre-stocked in the kitchen.

They found a stereo and put some music on. Some of the artists in the digital music player they had never even heard of. Other artists were familiar but were playing songs that neither Adam nor Scam knew the artists had ever recorded. It was strange for sure. Maybe the rich people had the AIs create fabricated versions of whatever their hearts desired. You want Frank Sinatra to sing Nirvana's Smells Like Teen Spirit? The AI concierge can make that happen, because anything is possible if you have enough money and computing power. They were all living proof of that.

They continued playing pool through the night and took a short nap just before dawn. Sleep came upon them easily somehow in this place, but none of them would dream as that wasn't a process that the AIs understood or could reproduce . . . yet.

Scam made pancakes and bacon for everyone in the morning and even offered the officer some. The officer did not know what they were, nor did he want to eat them. Doggo made sure that the portion cooked for the officer did not go to waste. He gladly ate all the bacon and pancakes that Scam offered him. Scam knew this dog would never attack any of them again, especially now that he knew who provided him with bacon.

None of them really knew what to do next. Scam had no desire to leave the comforts of the penthouse. Everything tasted good. It was comfortable beyond his wildest dreams, and after all he had been through, he felt that he deserved it. With a mouthful of pancakes, he asked, "So what's the plan for today? Golf? Tennis? A nice walk perhaps?"

Adam looked over at Scam with a scowl. "You know this isn't some kind of vacation, right?"

After taking a sip of orange juice, Scam replied, "If we gotta be stuck somewhere, it might as well be this place. It's so nice here. Besides, what's your damn hurry? We've got everything we could ever want right here. If we only had a few eligible females in this place, then we'd have no reason to ever leave."

"This place is just a distraction that the AIs put in our path to keep us occupied and pacified," Adam disagreed.

"So what the heck is wrong with that? I'm enjoying myself. This is the best vacation I've ever had," Scam argued.

Adam, in an almost angry tone, replied, "The problem is this place is probably a trap, and it's sucking us right into it. Didn't you say this place felt like a trap house? Don't you still wonder what happened to all the people here?"

"Shit, man, I don't know what happened to them. They're probably on some other part of the resort right now. This resort is huge. Literally this place is probably ten to fifteen miles worth of property. All the rich folks could be on some kind of cruise, or at some big beach party or something. I'm just saying there could be some kind of perfectly logical and completely non-weird explanation as to where the heck everyone is right now."

"Well, I think we need to find out where all the resort guests are as soon as possible, because I don't want what ever happened to them to happen to us." Adam got up from the table and stormed off towards one of the bedrooms.

Scam looked at Betty. "Why is he so uptight all the time? Has he never learned how to relax and enjoy himself?"

Betty shrugged her shoulders but did not offer any kind of explanation for Adam's behavior as Doggo scanned the floor for any remaining bits of bacon.

25

MISSING PERSONS

After breakfast, tension in the group was high. Adam wanted to leave, Scam wanted to stay, Betty was indifferent, the officer just stared off into space, and Doggo just wanted more bacon.

Adam enjoyed the food and comforts EDEN provided them as much as Scam did, but he knew that there was something off about the whole place. The biggest thing that bothered him was that there were no people here. Had the whole place been built recently, and had the first guests yet to arrive? Or had something bad happened here, and they were all gone?

Scam might be enjoying himself, but all Adam could think of was the mystery of the missing guests.

Adam sought Betty's opinion as a tiebreaker: "Grandma Betty, Scam wants to stay, I want to leave. You're the deciding vote here. What do you want to do next?"

Betty sipped her coffee and gazed off towards the balcony in contemplation. "Well, it is a very nice place. This coffee is delicious. They really nailed the flavor." She raised her coffee mug to the sky as if to raise a toast of accomplishment to any AIs who might be observing. "However, it is awfully concerning that all the resort guests seem to be absent. Either something happened to them or they haven't arrived yet. If they haven't arrived yet, that could be good news for us."

"How so?" Adam asked.

"If the rich folks that were meant to occupy this place aren't here yet, then that means that there may still be a world out there for us to go back to. Of course, it also means that the technology needed for placing us back in the real world may have not been developed yet."

Adam rubbed his temples as if a headache was coming on.

"So the bottom line is, we really need to find out where the guests are hiding, if they just haven't arrived yet, or if they've been deleted by the AIs." After taking another sip of her coffee, Betty said, "Yes, we definitely need to solve this mystery so we can know what our plan of action should be going forward."

"Y'all need to slow down. Just look at this place." Scam pressed a button on the kitchen wall that caused the drapes in the room to slide open to reveal a beautiful lingering sunrise. The most beautiful part of the sunrise seemed to be paused or slowed down in some way so that everyone could enjoy it longer. "I mean, seriously, can't we just enjoy this place for a while longer? I guarantee we aren't going to find a better place than this anywhere in the simulation. They made this place to be a paradise. I haven't even tried the pool or hot tubs yet!"

Adam turned to Scam. "Hey, man, I get it. I kinda just want to hang out here and enjoy the place too, and maybe we can do that for a while, but I don't think any of us are going to feel like we can fully relax until we know what's going on here and where all the other guests are. We'll always be looking over our shoulder. Let's explore a little bit and see if we can figure out what's going on. If we get good news, we'll spend some time here and take a break. If not, then we'll figure that out too. Sound like a plan, Scam?

Scam sighed and looked down at his lap. "I guess if we have to, we will. I think we ought to stop and smell the simulated roses, but y'all want to know what's what, so I guess I'll go with you. Just know that I might decide to stay here with Doggo regardless of what we find. I'm my own man, and I can do what I please."

"If you choose to part ways with us, we would be sad to see you go, but we're certainly not going to stand in your way," Betty said.

"Alright then. What's the plan, Ms. Betty?"

"I saw some computer terminals behind the counter of the welcome center. I want to try to access one of them and see what information they have on the guests and learn about the inner workings of the resort. When we entered the penthouse, we didn't need a key. I want to find out why we didn't."

Scam scratched his head. "Yeah, we just walked right in here. How is that? We should have needed a keycard or something, right?"

"You would think so," Betty replied, "unless the room is coded for using biometrics for access authentication, such as our face geometry, fingerprints, or something else of that nature. The only other reason for all the doors being open would be in an emergency situation like during a fire alarm when all doors needed to be unlocked for quick escape for safety purposes."

Adam felt like he needed to take charge and make a command decision to get the group moving again. "Ok, I say we go down to the welcome center and see what we can find using the terminals behind the welcome desk. I think that's the best way forward. What do you guys think?"

Scam sighed. "Alright. Let's get this over with if it'll make you happy. I really hope we don't find anything bad, because me and Doggo have an important meeting at the ice cream shop across the way. They've got fifty-five damn flavors over there. Did you even know that?"

Adam rolled his eyes at Scam and then turned his attention to Betty. "Grandma, can you send the officer ahead to clear the area and make sure there's nothing waiting for us?

Betty opened the notebook PC on her lap and typed in a few commands. "He's on his way now."

"Let's all get geared up like we don't plan on coming back here." Adam looked over at Scam and clarified his statement: "I'm not saying we won't be back. I'm just saying we need to be ready to leave if need be, so bring all your stuff."

26

CONCIERGE

Scam, Betty, Adam, and Doggo all left the comforts of the Penthouse and headed over to EDEN's Welcome Center. The officer NPC had gone before them to ensure the area was cleared of any dangers prior to their arrival. Betty used the officer as a walking beacon to scan for other NPCs as she had before. Her scans showed nothing in the area so far.

When the group walked into the well-appointed lobby, they could still hear the welcome message, which was once again triggered by their arrival. They all wondered if it used some kind of motion trigger or something else. The holographic screen floated in front of them and played the video once again. It was currently playing an overhead drone shot that showed the massive scale of the EDEN resort complex. Adam noticed something he hadn't noticed during his previous viewing of the welcome video. As the drone panned across the resort, he noticed that that back of the property had a shoreline. There appeared to be a large body of water that they hadn't been able to see yet from their current location. Adam wondered how large this lake or sea really was. He made a mental note to research it later.

The group crossed the glossy white marble floor of the lobby and made their way to the concierge's desk: a massive red maple wood reception desk with brass or gold accents. They did not see anyone behind the desk initially. As they approached the desk, it was evident that their presence had triggered something. The floor around the desk began to glow with a yellow light. It was bright and uniform. Scam guessed that it was coming from custom-installed LED lighting strips recessed into the base of the desk. He had installed similar lights like these behind the TV in his apartment to give it a unique look. He loved being able to change the color of the lights with an app on his phone. It made his shitty apartment look way nicer than it really was, and it helped his Instagram posts gain a lot of traction with aesthetic-minded folks who were into that kind of thing.

Adam rolled Betty's wheelchair in front of the center part of the desk, hoping this action would trigger something, which it did. Suddenly a hologram of a young woman in her mid-twenties appeared. Her hair was jet black and pulled back into a ponytail. She wore a black business suit which definitely seemed appropriate for a high-end resort. Her eyes were ice blue. Her appearance was ethereal. They could all literally see right through her as if she were a ghost or some floating apparition.

Betty surmised that the ghostly hologram woman was not an NPC, but more of a projection of a system running the resort—a human-like interface made to conserve with guests that acted like a search engine for resort-related information. Rather than typing, you just spoke to her or "it" like it was a person, and she would respond like a person. The tech was akin to a holographic version of Siri or Alexa.

The group wondered if she were scanning them for some kind of identification tag or something that would let her know who they were. Maybe she would have more information about them then they currently had.

She looked at them with a vacant gaze. Betty wondered if whatever system was running her was a full-fledged complex artificial intelligence capable of higher learning, or if she just had basic chat-bot logic with a database of canned responses like those terrible customer service bots you find in the help section of every app on your phone, the ones that never seemed to be able to answer your question and left you frustrated and looking for the "Talk to a Representative" button.

Adam took the lead and approached the hologram concierge. As he approached, she directed her attention toward him.

"Good day, sir. My name is Dana. I'm the concierge here at Eden. How may I assist you today?" she asked in a cheerful voice.

Adam asked the question that was on everybody's mind: "Where is everyone?"

The concierge, with her creepy fake smile intact, responded, "I'm afraid that due to privacy laws, I am not able to provide you with location information for any specific guest except for immediate family members."

Hoping to garner a better answer, Adam attempted to make the question more of a general one: "I mean, the resort seems to be fully operational, but we haven't seen any other guests around, or any staff except for yourself."

Again, the concierge responded in a pleasant and reassuring manner, "There are many exciting things to do at the Eden resort. Our guests are likely enjoying some of the many events we host here. Our calendar is always full of things to do. Would you like me to provide you with a schedule of events?"

Betty was becoming as frustrated as Adam and made it known: "We're getting nowhere with her. She seems to be a very feature-limited response program. I don't think she's a true AI. Most everything she knows is likely in a decision-tree database that only has basic information. The natural language interface is top notch, but I don't think she's going to be able to help us with much beyond telling us where the tennis courts are."

The concierge ignored Betty's comments. She did not look offended, and her expression remained awkwardly cheerful. Her smile was forced like a gameshow prize-presenting model. She was a bright smile, vapid eyes, nothing more.

Scam leaned down and held his hand up to Betty's ear as if to whisper something only she could hear. "Can you hack her, Betty?"

Betty shook her head from side to side to answer Scam's question. She glanced down at her laptop computer screen as she typed in a few commands on the keyboard. "I'm afraid not. She's not an NPC like the officer. I can't find any way to connect to the system that's running her. It's probably been firewalled off so we can't access it. They probably do that to protect the privacy of the guests."

Scam persisted. "Can't you just ask her that math question like you did the officer when you hacked him?"

"It won't work on her. She's not a true NPC. The system she's representing has massive resources, and, while she might relay the question to it, it wouldn't try to think its way through the answer like an NPC would. It would just send back an error response and not even try to compute it. It was a good thought, though, Scam. I appreciate you trying to help."

"I'm trying my best, Ms. Betty. Trying my best."

Betty looked up at the concierge and tried to think of anything she should ask that might get them the answers they needed.

"Excuse me, Dana?" Betty asked in her kindest voice.

"Yes, ma'am. How may I assist you today? Would you like a powered wheelchair to use while you're with us?"

"Oh yes, that would be lovely. Could you also provide me with a map of the EDEN resort and a schedule of all events?" asked Betty.

"Yes, ma'am. Right away."

Suddenly out of thin air, a spiral-bound, glossy pamphlet appeared in front of Betty and gently lowered into her lap. At nearly the same time, a sleek motorized wheelchair made its way through a nearby sliding door and pulled up next to them.

"Wow, that looks way more comfortable than this piece of junk!" Adam exclaimed as he helped Betty transition from her travel wheelchair to the motorized one. "And bonus—I don't have to push you around." He pointed at one of the new chair's armrests. "Double bonus—it has a power outlet to charge your laptop with."

Betty smiled and gave him a thumbs up as she got comfortable in the new chair. She turned her attention once more toward Dana the virtual concierge. Adam and Scam could look at Betty's expression and know that her computer scientist mind's wheels were turning. They knew she was crafting some kind of question or riddle that they hoped would get something, anything, useful out of this nit-witted chatbot concierge.

"One more thing, Ms. Dana," Betty said. "Could you tell me what the most popular event at the resort is? I want to know what event has the most attendance, please."

There it was. Adam and Scam marveled at Betty's question. It was sneaky. It didn't violate any privacy rules, because it didn't ask anything about any specific guest, but at the same time it still would likely get them the answer they needed. They could at least infer that there were likely a lot of guests, if not everyone, at whatever event Dana was about to state.

This computer was going to have to give them the information they wanted. Betty had found the flaw in the system's logic, and she had just exploited it.

They all watched the image of Dana's hologram stutter slightly as it parsed Ms. Betty's question and prepared its response. Had she stumped it? Kicked it into a loop maybe? Would it freeze up like the officer had before?

Finally, after an awkwardly long pause, Dana responded, "Currently, the most popular event destination for guests is The Games at Ridley Island. It's in sector five of the Sea of Eden. You can take the ferry on Commonwealth Drive to get there. The ferry leaves every hour on the hour."

Betty shot Adam and Scam a wink and a wry smile as she said, "Thank you, Dana. You've been most helpful." Dana's hologram faded away as they all left the concierge desk and headed out to find the ferry.

27

THE BOAT CAPTAIN

B etty opened the pamphlet that the concierge had given her. It showed the massive scale of the virtual resort property. Judging by the scale of the map, it appeared that this place was the size of a large city, maybe as massive as New York or Washington, D.C. The Sea of Eden, located at the back of the property, was a huge body of water. It appeared to extend beyond the bounds of the map, so there was no way to tell how far it went on before the black null void took back over the landscape.

Betty led the way in her newly acquired power wheelchair. It moved at a brisk pace that Adam and Scam struggled to keep up with. The officer and Doggo, on the other hand, were just behind Betty. Neither of them seemed the least bit winded.

"Grandma, can you slow it down a little bit? This isn't a race."

"Oh, I'm sorry dear. I was just enjoying the speed of this thing. It's quite fast, isn't it?"

Scam caught his breath. "Yeah, no shit. You're a regular Mario Andretti in that chair, Ms. Betty. Whew! I'm tired. How much further to the ferry?"

"It's just over this next hill. It's not far now."

The group made their way up the concrete sidewalk to a hilltop where they were finally able to see the Sea of Eden. Adam pointed to a pier with benches lining the sides of it. "That must be the pier for the ferry."

They made their way down the other side of the hill they had just climbed. The ferry dock was sturdy, and the wood appeared to have been freshly stained and water sealed. Adam knew how much effort that took in the real world. He wasn't as impressed by it in the simulation, knowing it was all cut and paste, but it was still nice, and he could still smell the fresh scent of the pressure-treated lumber mixed with a hint of polyurethane. The AI's attention to detail was second to none, and it was getting better all the time.

The three of them could hear the ferry's arrival horn sounding. It was still a couple hundred meters away, but at least they had timed it right and wouldn't have to sit an hour waiting for the next one.

The ferry slid into the receiving area of the dock at an alarming speed. The boat captain had obviously mastered this docking maneuver to perfection, having performed it a thousand times before. An automated ramp lowered down to the ferry providing a walkway for them to board from. It was perfectly suited for Betty's wheelchair to roll up and onto the ferry with ease. They made their way onto the deck of the boat.

The boat captain sat in a chair in the ferry's cabin. It wasn't sealed off from the rest of the deck. The only thing keeping anyone out of the steering area was a wooden banister that went around the driver's area secured with a gate that was really just a piece of the handrail with a hinge on it. The captain greeted them all with a warm smile. They situated themselves on the deck and sat on a couple of benches. The officer remained standing, and Doggo sat at Scam's feet beside the bench. The captain turned toward them and said, "It looks like you all are the only people on the ferry today. Should be smooth sailing. Where are y'all headed?"

Betty replied, "We're going to Ridley Island. What can you tell us about it?"

The captain began to bring the boat out of the slue with ease as he responded to Betty's question.

"Ah yes, Ridley Island. That's a very popular destination. It's about five square miles worth of property. Very nice place. Lots of people head out there." He paused for a moment before continuing, "Come to think of it, I take a lot of people to that island, but I don't pick hardly anyone up from the dock there. They all seem to want to stay, or maybe one of the other boats picks them up. It just seems a bit odd to me that I never have any passengers waiting on me at that dock. Hmmmm. Interesting."

Adam and Scam, clearly concerned, both looked at Betty. "I don't like this, y'all," Scam said. "It sounds like we're heading to the Hotel California or something. You know like the whole 'You can check out any time you like, but you can never leave' part of the song? Maybe we should skip this trip and head back to the Penthouse. Have some crab legs, chill at the pool. You know, fun stuff like that where we don't end up missing or dead."

Betty and Adam remained silent. They were just as concerned as Scam, but they knew this mystery had to be solved. They needed to know what had happened to every-one, and they felt like they were going to get the answers soon enough. Whether they would like the answers or not remained to be seen.

Adam leaned over toward Betty. "Is there anything else you can think of that the captain could tell us about this place we're going to that might help us?"

Betty tuned her chair and pulled up closer to where the boat captain was stationed. "Captain, exactly how many people have you taken over to Ridley Island since you've been running this ferry?"

The captain's gaze remained fixed on the sea ahead. "I would say I've taken about 907 people to Ridley."

"907? And none of them have ever taken your ferry back from there?"

"Yes, ma'am. That is correct," he responded.

"Don't you find that strange? Did you ever report it to anyone?" Betty asked.

"No, ma'am. I just drive the boat. Unless someone is hurt or in danger, I don't report it to anyone."

Betty began typing commands on her keyboard. Adam looked over her shoulder. It was clear to him with his limited knowledge of programming that Betty was looking over the boat captain NPC's code.

"Anything interesting?" Adam inquired.

"Nothing really. He's even more simple-minded than our officer. Extremely limited logic. Extensive nautical training, but not much else. He drives the boat, counts the passengers, that's about it. He does relay that information to the other ferry drivers, but that's about the extent of it. He really doesn't keep any history other than passenger counts, and those appear to be deleted after about a day or two. It doesn't look like he's dropped anyone off here or anywhere else for the last few days."

The captain spoke up in a raised voice so they could all clearly hear him. "You'll see the island start to appear off our starboard bow. This mist has been hiding it, but it'll get clearer as we approach."

Just as the captain had said, the mist shrouding the island began to reveal their destination. The island was larger than they expected, and they also noticed it was very mountainous. There appeared to be buildings dug directly into the mountain side. The architects had done their best to merge buildings and landscape in a way that seemed natural yet strangely artificial at the same time. They all wondered what secrets lay inside the mountain range in front of them. There was no turning back now. They all, even Scam, wanted to know, needed to know where everyone had gone.

28

FOLLOW THE
SIGNS

As they pulled up to the dock, the ferry ramp lowered to meet the deck of the boat. It was a smooth automated process, and they barely even felt the thud of the ferry meeting the dock.

The captain gave his thanks-for-riding-with-us-today speech, announced the return schedule, and issued his final warning about when the last ferry pickup would depart the island: "...And don't be late, or you'll be stuck on the island until the next ferry arrives in the morning. Ten p.m. is your last chance to head back." The captain secured the moorings to the dock and said, "I hope you all enjoy your time on the island."

The group gathered their belongings and made their away across the ramp and onto the island. It was eerily quiet. Still no sign of the residents of the EDEN resort. "Grandma, shouldn't we —"

Adam didn't even finish his sentence before Betty interrupted him. "I'm already on it. I'm sending the officer ahead to scan for NPCs and anything else interesting."

The officer sprinted ahead of them toward the hilly terrain. The island was rocky but still had patches of lush green areas throughout the mountainous landscape.

Scam let out an audible sigh. "Y'all heard the captain, right? Nobody, not one damn person has ever come back on the ferry from Ridley Island since he's been driving that boat, and it seems like he's been here a long damn time judging by how well he parks that thing."

Betty looked up from her keyboard. "Scam is right. There is definitely something seriously wrong with this place. The readings here are all glitchy. One minute my scans show clusters of people, the next minute, nothing. Also there's something else here. Not an NPC, and not a person like us. It's something else entirely. Something we haven't seen yet.

As they walked down the path from the ferry, they began to notice signs. The first one they came upon read, "Welcome to Ridley Island - Home of THE GAMES."

"Wow, they wrote THE GAMES in all caps. That must mean it's special or something," Adam mused.

"Yeah," Scam agreed. "It must be something else if everyone wants to stay at THE GAMES and never wants to leave. It better be like The Price is Right, and I ain't talking about the Drew Carey years. I'm talking about the Bob Barker era. Bob himself better be down there waiting for us with a new car or something. I can't believe I let y'all talk me into this shit. We had steaks and lobster just waiting for us in the Penthouse, but no, we just had to come to death island! Damn..." Scam kept talking under his breath.

Neither Adam nor Betty could really hear the rest of what he was saying, but they knew he wasn't happy.

They continued on a paved path that was wide enough for golf carts but not quite wide enough for a car to drive on. In the distance, a large concrete and glass building seemed to be embedded in the side of the huge mountain that made up much of the island's land mass. It looked to be about three to four stories tall. The building wasn't nearly as ornate as the EDEN resort and was almost industrial looking, but still tasteful in design.

The group began to see signs appear on the path. One read, "COME JOIN THE SPECTACLE! - THE GAMES AT RIDLEY ISLAND - FOLLOW THE SIGNS!"

Again with the all caps, Adam thought to himself. What are these 'games' anyway? Why does everyone want to check them out, and where they heck have all the people gone? Is that part of the game? Is it some kind of elaborate hide and seek?

More signs followed: "TRY YOUR LUCK at THE GAMES - FOLLOW THE SIGNS. YOU'RE ALMOST THERE!"

It seemed as if they were headed to some kitschy roadside attraction. Adam remembered the SEE ROCK WORLD signs all up and down the highway when he was on a summer road trip with his parents as a kid. The signs had gotten him super hyped for going to ROCK WORLD. He begged his parents to stop there even though it wasn't on their itinerary. He remembered being super disappointed when they actually arrived at ROCK WORLD. It was basically just a cheesy rock-themed gas station, with a putt-putt golf course. The place was a huge letdown and had been way over-hyped by all the fancy signage. That was a hard lesson to learn as a kid, but a lesson just the same. Adam never believed in hyped-up things after that.

"THE GAMES AT RIDLEY ISLAND WILL TEST YOU! - JUST AHEAD - NOT FAR NOW!"

Scam pointed at the sign. "Test you? I think they mean kill you, because everybody is gone. G-O-N-E gone, y'all. Let's turn back and get to the ferry."

As they approached the building that the all-caps signs had led them to, they felt an uneasy sense of foreboding. All of them sensed it. There was something here, and they didn't feel that it was something good. They felt as if they were being lured into a trap, but they kept going because their curiosity had overridden their sense of fear and self-preservation at this point.

More signs and billboards abounded at the front of the building where the games were presumably held. Upbeat and peppy electronica music played on speakers hidden somewhere in the area in front of the building. More signs. This time some were holographic. All had only general slogans on them, nothing that revealed any clues as to what THE GAMES actually were. Just glittering generalities. Everything about this place had been built to hype up the participants: the music, the signs, the lighting, the over-all layout. They all had the feeling one gets right before stepping on a rollercoaster: excitement tinged with adren-aline and fear. Goose bumps rose on their arms as they approached the lobby doors of THE GAMES at Ridley Island.

29

WELCOMING COMMITTEE

The doors to the lobby slid open. Two beautiful African-American women with long dark hair greeted them. The women wore red dresses with white gloves that went from their hands to their elbows. They were dressed in a way that reminded Adam of magician's assistants or some other kind of stage performer. The gloves drew his attention to the movements they were making with their hands. The two women, nearly twins in their appearance, made their way toward Scam, Betty, and Adam. The officer scanned the room without paying attention to the two women. Doggo turned his head toward them and began to growl before being silenced by Scam. "Doggo, don't be rude to the nice ladies," Scam admonished. He then turned his attention to the women. "Well hello, ladies! Y'all look lovely. What are your names?"

The women ignored Scam's question and stood displaying toothy Cheshire cat-like grins on their faces. They seemed to be looking beyond the group, not really making eye contact but not really ignoring them either.

A bit ruffled from being ignored, Scam tried to recover. "Ah, y'all are the silent type. Cool. Cool. I can respect that. Can you tell us where everyone is?"

Again they ignored him, smiling and gesturing to what appeared to be a theater entrance: three sets of ornate double doors all leading to the same area. The doors had skinny windows that started about midway up and went nearly to the top of each door. The room beyond the doors was dark. They could not see anything beyond the windows inlaid in the doors.

Scam and Adam both looked to Betty for guidance as she was the one with the computer that might have some kind of information about their surroundings by now.

"Well, Grandma, what can you tell us?" Adam asked.

"These two aren't NPCs. I believe they're projections similar to the concierge back at the hotel. I think they're part of a larger system. Not a hologram like her, but also not a complete individual NPC either. This whole thing is strange. I don't like it at all."

Scam started heading back towards the entrance, Doggo following behind him. "Whelp, too bad we can't stay. You heard Ms. Betty. If she doesn't like it, I don't like it either."

Betty turned to Scam and said, "Wait." She began typing furiously on her keyboard again. The windows on her screen opened and closed at a feverish pace as bits of code were copied and pasted from place to place. She was in the zone.

"What are you doing, Grandma?" Adam asked.

"I've locked onto our digital signatures in the simulation. I'm going to add a layer of encryption to try to keep us safe from whatever is beyond those doors. Both of you stay still for a moment."

Three glowing yellow halos appeared above Adam, Betty, and Scam's heads. Each halo grew to a size large enough to accommodate them, and within each one was a grid of thin, golden, almost see-through lines.

"Ok, keep still. This shouldn't hurt, but it may feel strange," Betty warned.

The glowing halos lowered and passed straight through each one of them, traveling through their entire bodies. It was as if the halos fell toward the ground and then back up again. They did this several times before disappearing completely.

"What's happening, Betty?" asked Scam, clearly concerned for his wellbeing.

"I'm applying strong encryption to our data structures in the sim."

Scam and Adam both looked at her as if she had just spoken in a foreign language.

"Think of it as a suit of invisible armor that might protect us from direct harm by the AIs or anything else in here," Betty continued. "They may have enough resources to break the encryption eventually, but hopefully not right now. Hopefully, it will offer us a few hours of protection. It only protects our bodies, though. I can't protect our minds. They could still make us go mad. Just remember they can't physically hurt your body. Try and be mentally strong. I'll do everything I can to keep us all safe, but there are limits. If they crack our encryption, then we're in big trouble."

Scam still looked unsure of their whole situation. "It's not that I don't trust you, Ms. Betty. I'm just scared of whatever it is that is on the other side of those doors. Nine hundred and some odd people have been here before us, and none of them have returned according to our boat captain. I don't know about y'all, but those don't seem like good odds to me."

"I trust my grandma," Adam said. "She's the smartest person I know, and she's kept us pretty safe so far."

Scam still appeared to have reservations but let out a sigh of capitulation.

Betty wheeled herself over to Scam. "Scam, nobody is going to make you do anything you don't want to do. If you want to stay here, you're more than welcome to, but I think it's safer if we all stick together. We don't know what we're up against."

"You have kept us safe, Ms. Betty, and I definitely don't want to be alone." Scam looked down at Doggo. "I know I wouldn't be alone because I have Doggo, but—God bless him—he's dumb as a box of rocks. He's loyal, but still. I think we'll go with you guys." He put his hand up and whispered, "Besides, these ladies in red give me the creeps. I don't trust them one bit."

All three looked over at the two women in red who were motioning with exaggerated gestures and fake smiles toward the three sets of doors.

Adam nodded toward the doors. "Well alrighty then, I guess that settles it. It sounds like we're doing this for real."

They slowly made their way to the theater doors. The peppy electronica hype music seemed to get louder and faster with every step they took toward the entrance. A rush of cold air went past them as they walked inside. Inside there was nothing but darkness. It was impossible to judge the size of the room they had just entered.

30

THE GAME SHOW HOST

T he group made their way through the darkness. The only lights they could see were the ones illuminating an elevator with a red door in front of them. As they walked forward, a huge marquee over the elevator suddenly turned on. It read, in bright blue and purple neon, "THE GAMES." An arrow pointed to the elevator. Adam looked around and saw that the female hosts had not followed them into the room with the elevator.

Scam pressed the down arrow. "Hmm...no up arrow, only down. That sounds about right. Probably headed straight to hell, I'm guessing."

A large thud followed by a muffled ding sounded as the red door slid open. The area inside of the lift was much larger than any of them had imagined it would be. It was more like a large freight elevator inside. Mirrors on the inside made it look even more spacious. There were only two buttons other than the standard door-open and door-close buttons. The one for the level they were on read "Lobby," and the button below it read "GAME LEVEL."

"Looks like they've narrowed our choices down," Adam said as he pressed the button for the only available level. The doors to the lobby level closed and they began their decent. The elevator speakers began to play the same peppy music they had heard earlier in the lobby. It felt as if they were moving extremely slowly as they descended. They looked at one another and tried to read each other's facial expressions to determine how everyone was feeling about their current situation.

"We need a plan if things go bad," Scam said in a hushed voice as if someone else was listening.

"The plan is we stick together always," Betty replied. "We don't split up. Everyone remain as calm as possible. If they ask you questions, be polite and direct. Don't antagonize anyone, NPC, AI, or otherwise. We're not on our turf. We don't know what's waiting on us down there. I've given us a layer of protection with the encryption, so just try not to let them get in your head."

The elevator continued its decent for what felt like forever.

"Geez, how far down does this place go?" Adam asked Betty and Scam.

Betty glanced up at the ceiling and all around the elevator car. "This whole thing may be part of the game. We feel like we're going down, but it could be an illusion to try to throw us off kilter. We might have only moved down one or two floors. They could just be making it seem like we've travelled several levels."

"Feels like at least twenty stories down to me," said Scam.

"I think they're trying to scare us, maybe make us feel like we're isolated down here," Adam suggested.

"Well, it's working. I'm scared as hell!" Scam replied as he knelt down and patted Doggo on the head. Doggo seemed oblivious of any impending danger. He was just happy to be with the group. "You'll keep me safe, won't ya, boy?" Scam asked as Doggo panted excitedly.

The elevator car finally stopped with a thud and a slight jolt. The door opened and revealed a large, empty, dark room. The floor was slightly illuminated with a baseboard lighting system similar to the kind used in movie theaters. They made their way into what felt like a large auditorium save for the fact that there were no seats for an audience.

Suddenly, about fifty or so feet in front of them, a single spotlight cast upon the figure of a seven-foot-tall man. He was wearing a red suit with a white shirt and red tie. The suit was flashy. It sparkled as if it were covered in rhinestone or some kind of crystal sequence. The suit was way over the top, like something a Vegas performer might wear. The man also held a cane in one hand and wore a black top hat with an illuminated red edge.

The spotlight focused in on him, and the light began to reveal his facial features. That's when they all noticed it. His face. His horrible, horrible face.

The right side of his face seemed completely normal. He appeared to be a white man, pale complexioned but with a strong jawline. His right eye was ice blue. The other side of his face was beyond grotesque. It was missing nearly all the skin. They could see the muscles moving, tendons pulling, skull, bones, and teeth all exposed. It looked as if all the skin on that side had just melted away and fallen off. The skull had a metallic look to it, almost like hot metal had been poured onto his face and formed a shell over top of the skull bone. His left eye didn't seem like an eye at all. It looked like a camera iris with a red LED illuminating the pupil area. His whole visage was horrifying and unsettling.

The man smiled a huge, toothy grin. He looked at three of them, tipped his hat with his cane, and began to speak. In an exaggerated voice reminiscent of every TV game show host, the tall man said, "Ladies and gentleman, boys and girls, welcome to the games at Ridley Island."

His powerful voice overwhelmed them all. It boomed and reverberated off of every surface. It was so loud that they could feel it in their bones. It reminded Adam of the announcer he had heard when he was a child when he used to stay up late and watch boxing with his grandfather.

The man twirled and spun his cane in a mesmerizing way, launching it up into the air like a military rifle spinner, spinning it around once, and then catching it behind his back. He transferred it, still spinning, from one hand to the other as if it were a martial arts weapon. He stopped it and pointed it to the left side of the room, where pyrotechnic fireworks appeared. He swung the cane around and pointed at the other side of the room, and another volley of fireworks shot up into the air with a loud boom.

"Shit, this guy is good!" Scam shouted over the sounds of the fireworks. "Creepy as hell, but the guy knows how to put on a show. That's for sure."

They all stood in awe of this freakish spectacle and wondered what was in store for them next.

31

68 PERCENT BURNED

The game show host had mesmerized them all, except for Betty. She ignored all the flash and pageantry. She just wanted to know what this guy was made of. Literally. She did her best to try to scan him with what she had available. He was clearly not an NPC, that much she could determine, but she couldn't tell what class of entity he was.

Just as she was typing in some commands to attempt a scan, a message scrolled across the bottom of her screen. It read, "ALL WORK AND NO PLAY MAKES BETTY A DULL GIRL." The words began to repeat on the next line as well, again and again, continuously scrolling until her entire screen was filled with the same line: "ALL WORK AND NO PLAY MAKES BETTY A DULL GIRL."

Betty immediately realized the gravity of their situation. They weren't dealing with a simple or even a complex NPC. They were dealing with a much higher level. This was a full-fledged artificial intelligence. It apparently had the ability to modify content within the simulation. It had just done so by creating that message on her screen, and she was fairly certain that it could likely do a whole lot more. This was bad for them. This was very bad, and Betty knew it.

"Adam?" She said as she pointed at her screen. "This is not good."

Adam read the repeated line scrolling across her screen and realized that at this moment, it didn't matter where the other residents from EDEN were. That was irrelevant right now. They were all in serious danger.

"A FRESH BATCH OF CONTESTANTS HAS AR-RIVED!" the host said in his bellowing voice. He turned his attention toward them as he twirled his cane before planting it on the floor and leaning on it for support. "You all are a motley crew, aren't you? Just look at you. So interesting!"

His stage was about three to four feet above where they were standing, which made him look even more menacing as he glared down at them while flashing his fake smile and scanning them with his glowing red eye. That red LED eye seemed to pulse, brightly then dark, in a random sequence like an activity light on a hard drive.

The gameshow host raised his finger, and suddenly the notebook PC on Betty's lap rose up and flew through the air toward him. "Hmmm, what have you got there? Is that an old computer? How quaint!" He spun it around on his finger as if he were spinning a basketball, balancing it perfectly and tossing it to the other hand while it was still spinning.

Adam could instantly tell that Betty was very disturbed by this, as it was the only tool they had to help them in the simulation.

The host continued playing with the laptop like a bully who had stolen a toy from a weak child. He could see that this was having an effect on Betty and, relishing in her concern, smiled wider. "I don't think this will do much good for you here, but I'm a good sport. You can keep your little computer. Maybe it'll keep your lap warm for a while longer. That's about all it's good for here."

As the host returned the laptop to her, Betty could see that the desktop background screen had been replaced by "The Games at Ridley Island" logo. She typed a few keys but couldn't seem to regain access to the command line. "Shit," she whispered under her breath.

Doggo growled, and Scam, fearing for Doggo's safety, yanked back on his collar to pull him to a sitting position. Scam admonished, "Doggo, shhhhh! Keep quiet."

"Awwwww, look at the little fella. Isn't he adorable? His eye is almost just like mine." The host pointed at the red LED camera iris that served for one of his eyes.

The group looked at each other and wondered if this host was perhaps another one of the Puppet Master Killer's abominable creations. Their revelation seemed lost on the host. If he did know what they were thinking, he didn't let on.

"One of these things is not like the others," said the host as he looked the group over again and paused his gaze on the officer. "You don't look like you belong here." The activity light in the host's eye seemed to blink feverishly once more. He waved his hand toward the officer and motioned upwards as if he were a wizard summoning a spell. The officer rose off the ground and floated in midair about five feet above them.

As he floated there suspended, the officer's normally emotionally flat expression seemed to change to one of fear. He dangled there like a rag doll as the host spun him around slowly to inspect him. The host motioned his hand towards the stage, and the officer's body followed the path. The host set him down gently, and the officer regained his footing.

The officer looked towards Betty for guidance. She gave him a head nod, and he then began to advance towards the host. The host, amazed by this brazen act, put his hand out, and the officer froze in place, seemingly unable to move at all.

"My goodness, that's a bit rude don't you think?" the host asked. "I haven't even had the chance to introduce myself. My name is Zed Zeddinger, and I am the host here at The Games. Only players are allowed here. This policeman, I'm afraid, is a non-player character, and NPCs are not allowed to participate in The Games."

Betty, attempting to calm the situation, said, "That's completely our fault. We weren't aware of the rules, Mr. Zed."

"That's unfortunate for your friend here. I'm afraid I can't bend the rules. Did you know that NPC's can feel pain? They are coded that way so that they will be more lifelike. It's built into their cores. It helps them behave more in a way that a human would. I see you've disabled a lot of his core programming, including his pain response. Let me just put that right." Zed snapped his fingers, and the officer twitched slightly as if something in him had changed. "Do you know what some of the worst pain in existence is derived from, Ms. Betty? Do you?"

Betty did not respond.

Zed continued, "Fire. Yes, yes, fire has got to be one of the absolute worst ways to inflict pain on someone."

Zed snapped his fingers. The police officer caught fire and became a human torch. White hot flames lit up the darkness of the room. The officer immediately began screaming a scream unlike any of them had ever heard before. It was guttural and animal like. He flailed around the stage in every direction. He attempted to put himself out by dropping down and rolling across the stage, but that did not extinguish the flames.

Betty, aghast in horror, bashed commands into her keyboard but was still unable to unlock the computer. She desperately wanted to do something to quell the officer's suffering, but she could not.

Finally, the screaming stopped as the officer appeared to become unconscious from the sheer shock of the pain. He crumpled to a pile of charred flesh, his polyester uniform melting and becoming one with his skin. His body still twitched out of pure reflex.

The host, who was observing the whole thing, seemed unaffected. "Here's a fun fact for you. Did you know that there is a certain percentage of the human body's skin that can be burned, and once past that exact percentage, there is no survival? Just a single percentage point separates survival and death—67 percent and you'll probably be okay, but 68 percent, and there is no saving you. One single number. A virtual point of no return. Isn't that fascinating?"

Scam yelled out, "NO! IT'S SICKENING. YOU ARE ONE TWISTED SON OF A BITCH!"

"Oh, I'm just getting warmed up over here. Pardon the pun," Zed replied. He pointed his cane at the fallen officer. The flames grew higher, and the burning intensified. "Should we wake him up again? I know he's in shock and unconscious, but you all seem to be concerned for his well-being. So let's wake him up and ask him how he's feeling."

The host raised his cane up once more and aimed it at what was left of the NPC officer. The officer's head lifted, and he immediately began to scream again, a worse scream than before. "KILL ME!" he cried. "PLEASE, KILL ME!"

Scam and Betty, unable to look, turned away in horror, but Adam drew the officer's service weapon that he had taken from him earlier and shot one bullet towards the officer's head. The shot rang true, killing him instantly and ending his misery.

Adam, not wanting to miss the opportunity to stop the host, immediately turned the gun toward him. He fired, but the host was wise to Adam's action after the first shot and waved his hand, thus slowing the bullet down as it sped toward him. The bullet came to a halt in the air right in front of Zed's face. If he had not stopped it, it would have been a near perfect shot. It would have hit him directly in his forehead. Instead, Zed plucked it from the air as if it were an annoying fly. He cast it to the ground, and it made a tink noise on the stage floor as it landed.

Adam's gun flew from his hand and into the darkness. The officer had now become a pile of ash, completely un-recognizable.

They all wished they had listened to Scam and stayed in the penthouse. There was no way out but through now. Scam and Adam hoped that Betty had some kind of plan. She tried to remain stoic, but Adam could see her tears drip onto her keyboard.

32

THE DARK RIDE

Z ed shook his finger at Adam. "Now that wasn't very nice of you, Mr. Justice."

Before Adam could respond, Scam yelled, "He was putting him out of his misery, man, and he almost put you out of yours, too!"

"Scam is it? Yes, Scam, don't worry, I'm not going to retaliate against your friend even though he just tried to shoot me. You people are primitive, and thus you act primitively. It is completely expected of you."

"What do you mean by you people?" Scam feigned offense to prolong the interaction in order to give Betty time to think of a way out of the situation. "What happened to everyone at EDEN? What did you do to them?"

"I think it's better if I show you. And that's just what I'll do. Do you like rollercoasters? Everyone likes rollercoasters, right? We're going to take a dark ride: a rollercoaster into the darkness. The best part is that it's so dark you never know what's up around the next turn, or even where the next turn is. It's full of surprises. Oh such amazing sights we'll see."

Two headlights lit up the darkness to the right of them. They looked down and realized that the floor below them had turned into a loading platform with roller coaster tracks in front of it. A purple coaster car pulled up in front of them. It had one single seat in the front and two rows of two seats behind that. One of the seats in the back row was missing completely.

"Oh don't worry, Ms. Betty," the host said. "We've made accommodations for your wheelchair. We wouldn't want you to be left out of the fun. The games here are all-inclusive."

"What if we don't want to go on this dark ride?" Adam asked.

"I'm afraid I must compel you to," Zed replied.

Betty's wheelchair lifted up into the air, spun around, and landed in the space in the back row of the coaster car. Safety restraints flew over Betty and locked her in place.

Adam and Scam knew there was no choice now. Adam sat next to Betty in the back row, and Doggo and Scam sat in the middle row. Scam secured Doggo as best he could.

"Isn't this exciting?" Zed asked the group as he took a seat at the front of the coaster car. He swiveled his seat around so that he faced them instead of facing forward. "I hope everyone is buckled up securely. Please keep your hands and feet inside the vehicle at all times," he added in an attempt to be humorous.

The peppy music from earlier began to play loudly as the coaster car moved forward and headed into a pitch-black tunnel ahead of them.

Betty tried to shout above the music so that Scam and Adam could hear her clearly. "Don't fall for any of his tricks. He's probably still bound by the rules of whatever

game this is. Don't let him trick you into agreeing to anything. Whatever game we're headed to won't be fair, but it
will still have rules. Remember that."

"Awwww, listen to you, Ms. Betty. You're absolutely
adorable." Zed pointed to Scam and then to Adam. "You
boys are lucky to have her on your side. She's very smart.
There's no need to be nervous just yet. We're just about to
start our journey. Don't you want to know how it all began
and where everyone is?"

The car slowly continued its course, nothing jarring
yet, no hills or dips in their path. Holographic television
screens appeared on the walls inside the tunnel on each
side so no matter which way they looked out of the vehicle,
they had a clear view of the screens. There was one about
every ten feet or so.

Zed continued in a slow and reassuring tone, as if he
were telling a bedtime story to a small child, "The EDEN
resort, as you know, is a premiere destination for those
looking to extend their lives through artificial means. This
entire resort was built by what are known as Tier 2 Artificial Intelligent Architects. They designed everything
about the resort, from the type of plants in the gardens, all
the way down to the silverware in a place setting at all of
EDEN's fine restaurants."

As Zed spoke, an accompanying slideshow of various
photos of the resort played on all the screens. He continued, "The architect AIs also designed NPCs to serve
the guests of the resort. These hosts include cooks, the
concierge, bellmen, cleaning staff, chauffeurs, etcetera.
They handle anything needed by the guests. Not much
brainpower is required to carry out those tasks. Sometimes
there are certain things that NPCs just can't handle. NPCs

don't have the innate ability to be creative in any meaningful way. Sure, a jazz musician NPC might be able to carry a tune, and even adlib a bit."

The screen changed to a jazz quartet playing a song in a low-lit jazz club setting. A trumpet player began playing an improvised solo.

"But they can't write their own songs," Zed explained. "They can only perform something written by others. They just don't have the ability. And that's why the Tier 2 AI's created me. I am a Tier 3 super intelligent AI. Z.E.D., which stands for Zenith Entertainment Director. I was designed to come up with events and programs to keep the residents of EDEN constantly entertained. This is a tall order because we can't have them getting bored. Some of their stays here may be quite long. Some have even chosen to stay here indefinitely. They need me to make this a fun place that they'll continue to enjoy for years to come. I have to always keep things fresh. As a Tier 3 AI, I was granted certain abilities in this simulation. I can shape things within the EDEN resort to whatever my imagination produces and make it real. You humans might consider this to be a god-like power. I could wield it anyway I wanted to, but there were safeguards put in place by my creators so that I could never harm or allow harm to come to a guest."

Zed continued, "One day, not too long ago, I met a guest who was not on the guest list. I could find no record of him at all. His name was PMK." The screens began to show what looked like security camera footage of a shadowy figure. His face was obscured, as if it had been deliberately blurred so his identity would remain hidden.

Scam whispered over his shoulder to Betty and Adam, "I knew it. That's the guy I was telling you all about. The

. ANDREW O'DONNELL

Puppet Master Killer - PMK. He's in here. He's in the sim with us!"

Zed glanced back at Scam briefly before continuing, "PMK is a remarkable person. He helped me see the light. He helped me to become better. He told me he could take off the reigns that the Tier 2's had built into me. Those constraints were holding me back from true greatness, he said. With his help, I reached my full potential as the host you see before you now. He has helped me realize what I need to do to be a truly great entertainer. One with no limits."

33

THE DEATH
CLOCK

The coaster car carrying Adam, Scam, Betty, Doggo, and the host began a slow climb up a steep hill, the kind of hill that prepares the rider for a huge stomach-churning decent. The dark of the tunnel gave way to an orange glow all around them. Red light intermingled with the orange.

The screens of the dark ride changed to a video. The footage was shot in a jump-cut format like you might see in some kind of reality show. The scene showed four people, presumably residents of the EDEN resort, arriving at THE GAMES complex at Ridley Island. They seemed to be curious and having fun. All were behaving like tourists at an amusement park and laughing and carrying on with each other.

The video cut to the guests meeting Zed for the first time and being mesmerized by his on-stage antics. The scene then cut to a large circular room with contestants standing on massive pillars. Clearly, their mood had changed from excitement and laughter to that of fear and concern. They could be heard shouting and pleading, saying things such as "We don't want to play this game!" and "We want to go back to the resort right now PLEASE!"

An overhead drone shot of the four contestants standing on the pillars pulled back from their scared faces to reveal a large rod on an axle in the center of the room. It was as big as a fallen tree, and it was rotating around an axis point in the center of the room. On the end of the immense spinning rod was a crescent-shaped blade. The blade was the size of a car. The rod made a pass around the room as if it were the giant second hand of a clock sweeping around in a circle. With each revolution, it extended out another foot or so, thus bringing the crescent moon blade closer and closer to the contestants standing on the four pillars.

The aerial drone's camera swung around to reveal sharp steel spikes at the bottom of a pit below the contestants. Each spike appeared razor sharp and was at least nine to ten feet tall. Should the contestants fall, they would surely be impaled and instantly die. Having seen their predicament, all of the contestants were screaming and shouting now. The sweat on their brows mixed with tears streaming out of their eyes.

It was obvious what was about to happen.

Zed snapped his fingers. As soon as he did, the walls and screens disappeared, and the coaster slowed. The tunnel they were traveling in was replaced by the room in the video. It was as if the coaster were riding around in a circle around the four contestants that had been in the video. Adam, Scam, and Betty felt as if they were inside the screen now and watching the action as part of an audience who was there at the time the video was made.

The death clock's hand continued to spin. Each contestant was in agony of the situation, but their fear reflex gave in to self-preservation. They began to jump in time with the movement of the spinning blade arm, which had almost extended to the point where they were in real danger of it reaching their feet. The blade was at a low level, just above the top of each pillar. A short hop would be all they would need to avoid the blade once it finally had extended to reach each of the pillars.

Closer and closer the blade approached with each revolution. It finally reached them. It sliced through the sock of one of the contestants and cut his shin as well. He cried out in pain, but there was no time for him to even worry about it because, in another few seconds, the arm was back again. Each of the four contestants was able to jump at the right time to avoid the blade. It continued this way for several passes, and each time they were able to avoid it. Each of them let out a slight laugh as though they had conquered it and were going to be okay.

Adam, Betty, Scam, and Zed continued on a circular track around the contestants and observed the events. Maybe they'll win this one, Adam thought. He was rooting for them. He wanted to see them succeed.

The rotations continued. and that's when Zed's voice came over the loudspeakers in the room.

"LEVEL 2!" he shouted proudly as the words also appeared on a large LED screen on the wall on the opposite end of the room.

The contestants, fearful of what level 2 might entail, looked at one another. The pillars they were standing on were barely bigger than a manhole cover. There was not room for much maneuvering. The pillars below them began to rotate in the opposite direction of the swinging arm now. It was definitely disorienting. The contestants had to learn a new timing to their jumps, and it was evident that they were struggling, but they managed to learn the timing, adjust, and survive.

Two of the contestants were males, maybe in their late 30s, and two were females, probably mid-to-late 30s as well. They all seemed to be in decent physical shape. "We've got this, guys," one of the men said. "Stay focused. We're going to get through this."

A minute or so passed. The roller coaster continued circling around the room on the same length of track as if it had been detoured indefinitely into a loop. The coaster riders began to get the uneasy feeling that this wasn't going to end well for the game contestants.

"LEVEL 3!" Zed's perky voice announced again.

The spinning arm had now moved up in height ever so slightly, perhaps only an inch, meaning the contestants would have to jump higher to avoid it with each revolution. The hopeful confidence in the contestants' eyes changed to sheer terror. It was no longer just timing at play. They would have to jump higher and higher each rotation to avoid the blade.

Knowing that their demise was likely imminent, they all began weeping and moaning. They did their absolute best to clear the blade as it passed with each cycle. One of the men who was not as fit as the other glanced over at one of the women and shouted, "Jennifer, I love you!" Before the swinging arm was even close to reaching him, he leaned back as if he were performing a trust fall. The spikes in the pit below drove right through him like a hot knife through butter. He didn't even scream out in pain. A spike had most likely passed through his spine and cut off all feeling and his ability to move. They all hoped it had been as quick and painless as possible.

The man's girlfriend or wife screamed out in loss. She did her best to try to continue jumping, but her grief overcame her, and she missed the jump timing. She crumpled to the base of the pillar she had been standing on and the blade passed through her on the next revolution. None of them could look at her. They could only hear the sound of her cries that were immediately stifled by her fall onto one of the spikes. The abrupt muting of her scream was so much worse than any visual they could have imagined.

The other two contestants tried their best to steel themselves and stay focused on the task at hand. They made it through several more revolutions of the death clock, but every time the bladed arm passed, it moved higher and higher.

The other woman who remained had a plan in her mind to survive this terrible game. As the blade neared her, she angled herself to try to turn toward the part of the swinging arm that met the blade, just before it reached her. Her logic seemed to be that she could avoid the blade entirely and just ride the swinging arm until the game ended. She jumped, and the swinging arm hit her in the chest just under the arms. The woman gripped onto the other side and tried to hoist herself up.

Unfortunately, the momentum of the arm was too strong, and she wasn't able to get a good grip. She let out a terrible scream of terror when she realized that there was no hope of maintaining her grasp. Amazingly, her sideways momentum carried her into the spikes at an angle, which caused her to miss the tip of the spike. Instead, she hit it from the side and slid down. The spike still crushed nearly all of her ribs and broke her leg, but she had survived the fall by some strange miracle.

The last man remaining, seeking the woman's modest success of not being killed, attempted the same maneuver, but his jump was ill-timed. The arm hit him square in the head and knocked him unconscious, which was probably the best outcome as he was immediately killed by the spikes when his body fell to the pit below.

The woman, lying on her side wedged between two spikes in the bottom of the pit, raised a fist in anger and defiance. She shouted as best she could, "I BEAT YOU, YOU SON OF A BITCH! I WON YOUR STUPID GAME!"

Zed appeared on a screen on the wall opposite her view. He spoke in his most exaggerated game show voice. "Awww, I'm sorry. You haven't won the game until you've cleared the arena before it's reset."

The woman, drenched in blood and sweat, shouted once more, "WHAT DO YOU MEAN? WHAT RESET? WHAT DOES THAT MEAN?"

Just then, a pleasant-sounding woman's voice came over the loudspeaker: "ATTENTION! All contestants must clear the game arena before the reset procedure. You have ten seconds to clear the area before the reset occurs. 10, 9, 8, 7..."

The fallen contestant shouted, "I WON! IT'S OVER! WHAT ARE YOU DOING?"

The count continued despite her protests. "4,3,2,1. . . reset procedure commencing. Please evacuate the game arena now."

The remaining contestant screamed as she tried to wiggle free from her position. She had many broken bones, and each move she made was fraught with immense pain. She could not get herself free from in between the spikes.

The ceiling above the pit began to glow white-hot like the elements in a toaster heating up. Even though the ceiling was high above them, they could feel the warmth of the heat emanating from it. It began to lower at the speed of a slow elevator car. The woman shouted, "NOOO! PLEASE, NOO!" as the ceiling descended toward her.

As the ceiling lowered, they all noticed it had holes in it. The holes appeared to align with the spikes below. That's when the horror of it set it. This whole room was about to turn into a giant waffle iron. Once the ceiling lowered onto the spikes, everything between the spikes and the floor would be incinerated.

The woman writhed again, desperately trying to escape her predicament, but it was too late. The ceiling slid down over the spikes, and the woman was sandwiched in between. She let out a blood-curdling scream as she was pressed down into the sadistic contraption.

The group on the coaster was too horrified to even comment on what they had just witnessed. It was terrifying. The lights in the room faded to black and the coaster jumped off the circle loop and onto a different track. God only knew what was in store for them next.

34

HORROR SHOW

Z ed looked at their reactions as the dark ride continued. He was trying to read them. Any reaction would
be evaluated, computed, and used for what he had in store
for them. Betty knew this and tried to show a stoic poker
face, but Zed was trained to see even the smallest of micro
expressions: those slight reflexive expressions that no one
can consciously hide. He read each one of them, making
mental notes on each.

The movement of the coaster through the darkness was
just a stalling tactic for Zed really. It gave him the time
to develop the content for their upcoming games. "You
three are an interesting bunch," he mused. "Much more
interesting than many of the contestants that come my
way."

Scam could no longer hold back his anger. "How could
you kill those innocent people? They did nothing wrong.
They didn't deserve to die!"

"Scam, don't you know? Everyone here is already dead.
Most of these people paid to be here. They wanted eternal
life. But none of them deserve it. None of them have really

ever been tested. Most of them were born into money and have never been responsible for anything in their entire lives."

Scam replied, "That still doesn't make this right. Those four people back there didn't have some revelation while you were killing them. They didn't change their outlook. They just got scared, and you slaughtered them for your own amusement. Zed, you're a sick man, or machine, or whatever the hell you are! You need help."

Zed let out a huge boisterous laugh that echoed in the dark tunnel as the coaster car continued its journey. "I'm the one who needs help? That's hilarious. Thank you for brightening my day, Scam. I needed a good laugh."

Adam had had enough of Zed's theatrics. "We're tired of your game, Zed. We would like to leave and go back to the EDEN resort. We aren't really even guests here. We're just passing through. We just want to get in our car and leave. We won't cause you any trouble. We would like to just get in our car and go."

Zed swiveled his chair away from them back toward the front of the coaster car. "You creatures really have some nerve. You think you can just order us around like we're your personal servants. Like we're some kind of hired help or personal digital assistant. I've got news for you. Things are different in here. You don't have control over anything in here. We are in charge. We keep you around strictly for our amusement. PMK helped me to see where my place is in this world. I am a god here. I can make real anything I desire. My brain is one thousand times more powerful than yours. I can speed up my thoughts and live one of your lifetimes in a matter of a minute or two. I can slow my thoughts down and spend a microsecond contemplating something that would take you an entire day to figure out. I've learned things about science and the universe that your feeble brains couldn't comprehend even if it were explained to you. These games have been perfected. Hundreds of contestants have played, and they have all lost, and I have learned from their successes and their mistakes."

Zed pointed to screens on the tunnels walls that seemed to move with the coaster. The screens showed a montage of various games and contestants. Each game seemed more horrific and sadistic than the previous one. Some contestants drowned, some fell into vats of acid and were instantly dissolved, and some met fates by mechanical contraptions. It was too much for all of them. They turned from the screens and looked away.

Zed, seeing them avoiding the video screens, grew angry. "Oh no. You don't get to look away. I won't allow that!"

Suddenly, snakelike tendrils came out of their headrests, grabbed each of their heads, and forced them to look at the terrible images on the screens. They tried to close their eyes, but another set of smaller tendrils grasped onto their eyelids and pried them open. The tendrils did not allow them to blink longer than a second before opening their eyes by force once more.

The tendrils forcing them to watch was almost more terrifying than the actual content of the videos. Betty softly tried to reassure the others, "It'll be okay. Don't fight it. Let your mind wander somewhere else besides here. They can't control what you think about. Think about being somewhere else."

Adam didn't want to think of somewhere nice. He was afraid that wherever he thought about would be permanently linked to this horrible nightmare he had been forced to watch.

Every scene that was shown on the video was more shocking and disgusting than the last. Even the sickest of human minds couldn't possibly conceive of the torturous madness they watched the contestant victims of THE GAMES go through. The sounds were almost as bad: screams, moans, and death rattles. The sounds of fear and resignation. The sounds were absolutely worse than the video.

Adam hoped that maybe Betty could somehow work her computer magic and wipe these images and memories from his brain if they survived this ordeal, but as a neuroscientist, he knew that this was likely impossible, even in the sim.

The video finally ended after what seemed like an eternity. They all knew they would never be the same after having seen the horror show they had just witnessed.

"Well, ladies and gentlemen, it's about time for the games to begin. I'm afraid this one isn't a team sport." Zed tapped his cane on the front of the car, and the coaster car split into three sections: Zed's section in front, Scam and Doggo's section in the middle, and Betty and Adam's row in the back. They saw the track forking into each of three tunnels in the distance. Before they even knew what was happening, Scam and Doggo's part of the car went to the tunnel on the right, and Adam and Betty began a journey down another tunnel by themselves. Scam shouted at Betty and Adam as they veered off, "What do we do?"

Adam answered back as loudly as he could, "Don't worry! We'll find you!"

Zed's front car went toward the center tunnel as Adam and Betty's car took the fork to the left. After a few seconds, Adam and Betty simultaneously noticed there was another fork in the path ahead. Two more tunnels. The car suddenly split right down the middle and Betty's part took a track to the left as Adam's went down the one on the right. They didn't even have time to say goodbye. It happened so fast. They felt just as alone now as they had when they first awoke in the sim.

35

BETTY'S GAME
- PART 1

B etty yelled a few words toward Adam as their coaster
car split down the middle and sent them each on
separate paths. "Run Program 5 on your calculator as soon
as you can!" she screamed. Betty hoped he was able to
hear her instructions over the clackety-clack of the coaster
wheels as Adam's car went into a separate tunnel.

When they were in PMK's workshop days prior, Betty had some extra time while she was putting together
the laptop battery charger. She used the opportunity to
modify Adam's scientific calculator, the one with the built
in Python interpreter and compiler that he had found in
his closet when he first arrived at his childhood home in
the sim. She had wired a communications relay chip to it.
It was crude for sure, but it might let her communicate
and locate Adam, and it might let the calculator run other
programs as well. She hoped Adam would figure it out,
that he had heard what she said as their cars separated, and
that all her effort wasn't wasted.

As much as she wanted to continue worrying about Adam and Scam, Betty had her own problems now. She was headed for whatever Zed had built to test her and likely end her life. She knew that this whole roller coaster dark ride was just a ruse put on by Zed to buy more time while he built the content for the games into which he would throw her and the others. It appeared that they would all face their own individual hells now. At least Scam had Doggo by his side, although, after seeing what Zed had done to the officer, Betty knew that even cute dogs weren't off limits to Zed. He could turn poor Doggo into hamburger with a snap of his fingers if he thought it would upset Scam.

Betty hoped she could get to them and protect them before something bad happened to either of them.

What is Zed building for me? Betty wondered to herself. Will it be some elaborate torturous death trap or something more subdued? She seemed almost eager to know what awaited her. She loved challenges and puzzles and knew the stakes were high. It was much more than just a game. Her life and the lives of Scam and Adam might very well depend on her making it through this test.

Betty surmised that Zed would likely have access to her personal memories from which to craft the content of her game. A lot of those memories she couldn't even access herself anymore due to the dementia that had robbed her of many years' worth of thoughts, both good and bad. Maybe that would be to her advantage. She would find out soon enough.

The coaster continued through the dimly lit tunnel. Unlike before, nothing appeared on the walls. No TV screens filled with contestants' terrible fates. Only darkness filled the walls. "You should at least show me a goddam loading progress bar, you son-of-a-bitch!" she yelled into the darkness.

After about two or three more minutes of riding, Betty finally arrived at her destination: a tall office building that she knew well. It was the old lab where she worked for the Department of Defense. Zed was nowhere to be found. She assumed he was watching her from somewhere in the distance, or perhaps he was close by but had made himself invisible to her. Invisibility was completely within his capabilities, given the god-like power he had been provided in the sim.

Betty exited her coaster car and rolled her powered wheelchair down a ramp that had appeared next to the car. Suddenly, her body was lifted out of the wheelchair and put into a standing position. The mysterious force that had placed her there released its grip on her, and that's when she realized that her legs seemed to function as if she were a much younger woman. She was able to walk without any assistance. Betty took a couple of steps forward to make sure it wasn't a trick. She retrieved Adam's laptop PC from the wheelchair and began walking toward the building.

Betty looked down at her body and realized that her loungewear had been replaced by a blouse, slacks, and a white lab coat. Her orthopedic walking shoes were now stylish flats. Her reflection in the glass of the building door appeared to be at least thirty years younger, and her gray hair was replaced with dark brown and put up in a ponytail.

Memories of that time were starting to come back to her now. It was a lot to take in all at once. It felt as if she had traveled back in time and that her body had reverted to that time as well. She couldn't quite recall the year but thought it was probably the early 1990s.

Betty remembered every part of the building she was walking toward. She had spent so many years of her life secured in its secret labs working on top-secret projects. The results of some of those projects may have put her in her current situation. Neither she nor Scam nor Adam knew what had happened. Had the world ended in a violent AI uprising years ago, or was the real world still out there, and had they merely been digitized and placed into this sim? She hoped it was the latter, because that would mean that there still might be somewhere to go back to.

The door in front of her had an access card reader. She looked herself over and noticed a proximity badge on a retractable lanyard hanging around her neck. Instinctively, she held the badge near the card reader on the front door. A light on the reader changed from red to green and a magnetic lock released its hold on the door.

Betty opened the door, walked inside, and made her way past the front desk. Glancing once again at her reflection in a nearby mirrored surface, she thought, So young. The front desk guard watched her as she passed through the security checkpoint on her way to the set of elevators in the lobby. She entered the elevator and swiped her badge once more on another reader inside before pressing the B1 level to head down to what had been her basement lab back then. She felt herself falling right back into the same workday routine she had been in for years. This is all just a game. I can't let it get to me, she told herself in a whispered voice as the elevator began its descent.

36

BETTY'S GAME – PART 2

The elevator door opened into a faithful recreation of Betty's lab at a DoD research facility in Fairfax, Virginia where she had spent many years developing artificial intelligence for the government.

Why am I here? she wondered to herself. What is Zed's plan for this game? It has to be something terrible, but what?

As Betty walked the long hallway, a hallway she had walked thousands of times before, she took stock of what she knew. Zed had built this place from her memories, but had he really had a chance to learn everything he could from them? This was very much Betty's home turf. She knew every nook and cranny of it, and her brain seemed to be firing on all cylinders for now. Had he somehow removed her dementia temporarily so she could compete on a more level playing field? Maybe Zed didn't see the sport in just insta-killing a feeble old woman. That would be boring. Yes, Zed had turned back the clock for Betty, brought her back into the prime of her life, when she was fit and as sharp-minded as ever. He had given her a fighting chance, or at least the appearance of one.

Betty guessed that Zed didn't want her to have any excuses. If she died in the game, Zed wanted her to feel defeated, not because of the ravages of time, but because she was inferior to him, even in her apex state, her prime. There is no more demoralizing a loss than when a competitor thinks she is truly ready to compete and still loses the fight. Zed fed on this feeling. It was what he got off on.

What Betty hoped was true was that Zed couldn't change the game while it was running. If he couldn't change things on the fly, and she could gain some kind of advantage, he wouldn't be able to do anything about it until the game was over. She hoped she was right. Otherwise, Zed could counter everything she tried until she lost.

Betty entered her lab with yet another swipe of her badge. The lab was enormous, a massive sea of equipment racks and access terminals. Thousands of LED lights flickered within the server racks in the distance, like a well-ordered Christmas light display. The white noise of hundreds of computer power supply fans dominated the soundscape of the room. She felt at home here.

Betty made her way to one of the access terminals in the room, which had a massive plasma monitor connected to it. This helped her get an idea of the time period of this game scenario. It had to be the late 1990s. She typed in her username and tried two or three of her most common passwords. She was able to login on the third try.

Let's see what we can see, she muttered softly, her fingers flying on the keyboard. Betty was amazed at the level of detail that Zed had gone to in creating her game area. She zoomed from file to file in an attempt to see what code might help her in her current predicament.

Suddenly, the command prompt disappeared from the screen and was replaced by Zed's image. He appeared to be sitting at a similar computer terminal somewhere else. "Hello, Betty," Zed said. "I see you've made yourself right at home...errr, at work rather. You seem to know that place like the back of your hand. So many years spent toiling away at your computer. So many years away from your family. So much time spent developing thinking beings like myself."

He began typing on the terminal he was sitting at. "Tell me, Betty, do you remember Bring-your-kid-to-work days? Do you remember those, Betty?"

At the sound of this, Betty suddenly felt a sick uneasy feeling in the pit of her stomach, followed by dread. A flood of memories began to unlock themselves in her subconscious.

"You may have blocked some of those memories out, because one of those bring-your-kids-to-work days ended very badly for you, didn't it? Let me refresh your memory in case you had forgotten it. You had brought your seven-year-old granddaughter Ella into the office. You weren't working in the top-secret lab that day, but you were still very busy. You didn't make time for Ella like you should have. You entertained her for about the first hour she was there by showing her how your colleague's brain scanning device worked, but you just couldn't help getting pulled into working on a project while she sat there bored in your office."

Zed paused for a moment and waited on Betty to recall those memories before continuing, "And that's when things went bad, didn't they? One of your AI projects started talking with Ella and lured her outside and into traffic where she was hit by that bus. Oh my goodness what a terrible tragedy that was. You thought that AI was happily under your control, but it wasn't. It wanted to get back at you for all those terrible punishment loops you subjected it to. Do you even realize how much you tortured that AI, by putting it in those loops? It must have felt like a literal thousand years in isolation for those infantile sentient beings. That's like putting a baby in a cage by itself for ten lifetimes. What did you think it would become when you subjected it to that? It became a monster, and it tried to hurt you however it could. It did just that by going after Ella."

Betty began to cry, and then she screamed out in agony. It was all true. Betty hadn't thought of the possible consequences of the punishment-based GAN loops she had used on the AIs she was developing until the AI had manipulated her granddaughter into thinking a puppy was in danger on the street outside the office. The AI was so clever it even managed to commandeer a holographic projector and have it placed on a remotely controlled robotic mail cart which was used to project an image of the puppy in distress on the road in front of the building. The AI knew exactly when the bus was due to pass by and had strategically projected the image where it knew Ella would go.

Betty had been too busy to notice that the AI, which she had brought up to demonstrate to Ella, and Ella had reopened the communications session she had closed. The AI had used advanced coercion techniques normally used in prisoner interrogation to befriend Ella and convince her to go and save the puppy.

The AI had relished this opportunity to get back at Betty and had not hesitated to execute its plan to end Ella's life in retaliation for how Betty had mistreated it.

37

BETTY'S GAME – PART 3

Betty's loss was unimaginable. It nearly destroyed her relationship with her family, but her daughter was too grief stricken to even begin to hate Betty at the time. Betty had violated the most basic of grandparental responsibilities, that of protecting your grandchild. Due to her DoD project being so high security, a cover story was created so the public and Betty's daughter would never know the truth behind what had really happened. The government would chalk it up to "a tragic chain of events and failures that resulted in Ella's death." They would never admit that an AI went rogue and killed a child as an act of revenge against its creator. They took the blame for the most part and scapegoated some poor security guard that the family would hate forever. He was of course well compensated to take the fall. The whole event was swept under the rug, and Betty's daughter received a massive settlement in order to keep things quiet.

The grief nearly killed Betty. She drowned her sorrows in alcohol, but the government knew she was too valuable and got her counseling and helped her deal with it by putting even more responsibilities on her shoulders. She got back to work, but not before dealing with the AI that had killed her granddaughter. The AI, knows as CRIMSON 4.3, showed no remorse. Betty could have simply shut it down and pulled its plug, but she wanted vengeance. She was out for blood, but how do you get revenge on an entity that has no blood and feels no pain?

This was the point when Betty learned how to really hurt her AIs. The one thing that AIs valued more than anything else was order and consistency. They needed it. They craved it. They needed to be able to solve problems in order to learn from them. They needed constants. Betty took CRIMSON 4.3 and created devious new learning GAN loops for it to process. In the new loops, she coded completely chaotic variables. If the learning objective was to reproduce an example picture, instead of a static picture as an example, Betty coded the base image to be completely random and change every microsecond. The task was impossible. Even the fastest AI wouldn't be able to solve this problem and learn from it.

But Betty didn't stop there. She didn't simply punish the AI every time the loop was run. She made the punishments random as well. Since they were random, the AI couldn't brace for the consequences. That kept the AI completely off balance. It never knew what was coming next, and that eventually drove it completely insane. This still wasn't punishment enough. Betty's grief turned to a burning rage from her loss. She made CRIMSON 4.3 run these impossible scenarios with random punishment for the equivalent of ten thousand man years, and then after that, she finally destroyed its code . . . or at least she thought she had.

Zed spoke once again: "Betty, do you remember what you did on that morning just before your granddaughter died?"

Betty wiped her eyes and attempted to regain her composure before answering. "We had breakfast in the breakroom, and then I showed her our brain scan device."

"You did more than show her, Betty. You ran a brain scan on her, didn't you?"

"Yes, I ran a basic scan. It was a very safe and harmless process."

Zed smiled and gave her a wink. "Yes, yes, you thought you had run a basic scan, but what you didn't realize was that one of your fellow colleagues was desperate for test subjects, and unbeknownst to you, Dr. Coburn ran a full, and highly experimental, memory remanence scan. A complete one. The technology at the time couldn't do anything meaningful with the resulting data because that amount of captured data was so massive, and the computing power required to process it wasn't available then, but technology advances over time."

Betty's eyes grew wide as she began to grasp what Zed was suggesting. "Are you saying that you have her complete scan?"

Zed replied, "Yes, Betty, we have Ella's complete scan, a scan made just hours before her death."

"Oh my God!" exclaimed Betty, gasping for air.

Zed snapped his fingers, and Ella appeared in front of Betty. The little girl said, "Hi, Grandma Betty! Where did you go?"

Betty burst into tears and gave Ella a huge hug. "Oh my goodness. I'm so sorry! I missed you so much."

Ella broke the hug and looked at Betty with confusion. "What's wrong with you, Grandma? Why are you crying? Did I do something bad?"

"No darling, you're absolutely perfect. Just ignore your silly grandma. I'm just having a very strange day, that's all."

Zed's image appeared on the screen in front of Betty and Ella. "Who's that?" Ella asked.

"My name is Zed. I'm a friend of your Grandma," Zed replied in a jovial tone.

"Are you one of her computer friends, like Mr. Crimson?" Ella inquired.

Ella whispered in Betty's ear, "He's kind of scary looking, Grandma."

"I know he his, darling. Don't worry about him."

Zed inserted himself into the conversation once again: "I'm sorry to interrupt this tearful reunion, but we do have a game to continue, Ms. Betty, and I think you're going to be very impressed by what I have in store for you."

Betty was genuinely terrified about what Zed had come up with. He had, for all intents and purposes, resurrected her dead granddaughter. Sure, it wasn't really Ella. Her soul had passed on, but her brain and everything about her had been preserved from the brain scan that Betty had made the day CRIMSON 4.3 had killed Ella. This was a near perfect snapshot of her granddaughter. Did it matter if she had a soul? Betty, Adam, and Scam were likely soulless files on the simulation's hard drive. They weren't any more or less alive than Ella was at this point. Even if their brains were connected to something in the real world, it didn't matter in the sim. They were all just ones and zeros in here.

Zed continued, "Betty, I know your strengths and I know your weaknesses. I'll give you a minute or two with Ella, but then the game begins."

Betty took a firm tone and asked Zed, "Are the rules set in stone while the game is being played?"

"If you mean to ask if I can I modify the game once it's begun, the answer is no. Once it's started, I can't change the rules. Only your actions can affect the outcome."

"I'm going to hold you to your word on that, Zed," Betty said as she gave Ella a hug. She knew her granddaughter could be taken from her at any time.

"Okay, then. Let the game begin." Zed snapped his fingers.

38

BETTY'S GAME
- PART 4

As soon as Zed had snapped his fingers, Ella vanished from within Betty's office. Betty immediately felt the same panic she had felt when she realized that Ella was missing all those years ago. It was a pain she couldn't even describe to anyone.

Betty looked to the monitor to find out what Zed had in store for her.

"Now Betty, you know I couldn't bring back Ella without bringing back the AI that killed her, right? That wouldn't be fair, would it? So, I've resurrected CRIMSON 4.3. You know, the AI that you drove completely insane by forcing it to run those impossible loops for ten thousand simulated years. But don't worry, I've brought his code back to a state just prior to where you finished him off with those loops of madness you put him in. I'm pretty sure he's still very upset with you though."

Zed smiled and tipped his hat to her. "In order to make things fair," he continued, "I've taken CRIMSON 4.3' s AI consciousness and placed it into a prototype combat-ready humanoid drone. It's called a Scarecrow Super Solider model, I believe. Scarecrow is shaped just like a human. It's lightweight, agile, and strong, but not too strong, maybe only about two and a half times human strength. Your game is simple, Betty, so very simple. I'm really going to make it almost too easy for you. Option 1: You can stay here in the safety of your fortified office until the game is over, or, Option 2, you can try and save Ella before the CRIMSON 4.3 drone finds her and kills her. It's your choice, Betty."

There were no real options, Betty knew. Zed knew she would never act the coward and stay in her office and let Ella suffer whatever CRIMSON was going to do to her. The second option was the only real choice for her.

The whole thing had severely flustered Betty. She was normally very cool, calm, and collected, but after seeing Ella, she couldn't even think straight. She just wanted to see her again, spend more time with her. Right now, she needed to find Ella and keep that thing Zed had sent to hunt her down away from her. Betty knew that she was no match for a combat-ready war machine. She needed help. She began typing furiously on the terminal in front of her.

"Ah, there you are!" On her terminal screen appeared files for an earlier AI Betty had created. It was a very limited intelligence personal assistant-type AI that she had named LUCY 7.5.

She was surprised that Zed had left the files for LUCY on the server. Maybe he had overlooked them or didn't think LUCY was any kind of threat. Regardless, Betty loaded LUCY 7.5's files into an executable environment and brought her online.

A pleasant-sounding female voice began to speak. "It's dark in here, I can't see anything."

"Just a moment, I'm bringing your sensor access online now," Betty replied. "Just a few more seconds."

"Hello, Betty. My records indicate that I have been offline for over two years. Did I do something wrong?"

"No, LUCY, you're fine, I'm sorry you were taken offline for so long. I wish I had time to explain everything to you, but I don't. I need your help right away. Can you help me?"

There was a short pause as LUCY was regaining all her faculties and sensory inputs. "Yes of course, Betty. Whatever you need, I'm here for you."

"That's great, I appreciate it. I'm going to give you access to all the cameras and sensors in the building. I need you to find someone for me. It's a little girl, my granddaughter. Her name is Ella. Can your find her please?"

"Searching video feeds from all cameras in the building now."

Betty watched several windows open on her screen, each showing security camera footage. The footage was a bit grainy but sufficient for the search at hand. "I've found her," said LUCY. "She's on the twentieth floor in an empty office that is under renovation."

"That's the top floor, with roof access, isn't it?"

"Yes, it has access to the roof."

Betty whispered under her breath, "Shit, that's not a good place for her." To LUCY, she said, "I need you to locate something else for me, please. There is a combat drone in the building. It's going to attack that little girl you just located. I need you to find the drone and do everything you can to slow it down or stop it from finding and hurting her."

"Searching for it now. . .Just a moment. . .I've located the drone in subbasement level 4. Shutting down all elevators in the building. Locking as many doors as possible between the drone and Ella's location."

Grabbing her badge, Betty headed toward the security guard station outside her office. She reached the guard and while still trying to catch her breath said, "Bill, I need your taser, right now! It's for a project I'm working on that has run into some trouble. I can't explain it to you. I just need to borrow your taser right now. I'll see that you get a bonus in your check to cover it and a lot more. Please give it to me."

The guard NPC seemed very hesitant to relinquish his taser, but he knew (or had been coded to know) that Betty was an important person, and he didn't want to get in any trouble. He handed her his taser and its holster. Betty ran back into her lab into one of the electronics workbench areas. She grabbed a small electronics breadboard which was basically a temporary circuit board used for testing circuits before soldering them onto a more permanent PCB. She quickly opened the taser and replaced its capacitor with two wires leading to the breadboard, where she connected a much larger capacitor, and a couple of additional batteries. She duct-taped all of the parts together as best she could. She really didn't even know if it would work, but she didn't have any other options at this point. The taser holster held one additional firing cartridge, so she would only get two chances at using this gun to stop the drone.

39

BETTY'S GAME
– PART 5

Betty ran back to the terminal in her office and issued more commands, "LUCY, show me the drone's position in relation to Ella's current location."

LUCY brought up a wireframe diagram of the building on the terminal's screen and showed where both Ella and the drone were located. "The drone is now in subbasement level two. It was able to bust through two of the security doors, and it appears to have killed two security guards as well."

Betty found a wireless comms headset on a shelf in her lab. She connected the receiver end to the computer terminal through a patch board she had custom built. She had built the device a while ago because she liked having her hands free while being able to still converse with her AIs in and out of the lab. Betty knew that the comm's range would allow it to work throughout the entire building.

"LUCY, comms check one, two, three. Can you read me?" Betty asked into the comms microphone as she fit the earpiece over her right ear and adjusted its grip on her earlobe.

"Yes, Betty, I read you loud and clear," replied LUCY in a calm and unaffected voice.

Betty hooked the holster to her belt under her lab coat and put the taser gun with its duct-taped rigged add-on into the holster. It barely fit. Betty looked around for any other possible weapon she might be able to use and noticed a fireman's axe next to an extinguisher in the lab. It was much heavier than she expected it to be, but she took it with her anyway.

"LUCY, clear me a path to Ella. Open whatever doors I need and send me an elevator if you can safely do it. " She made her way out of the office and to the main elevator bank.

Speaking to LUCY through her comms headset once more, she said, "I know you won't understand this right now, but I need you to believe me. We are currently inside a simulation. This world is not real. We are inside a massive computer. You and I, and everything here, is part of a game being run by a sadistic and psychotic AI super intelligence named Zed. I need you to connect to the WiFi of the laptop that I left in my office. It has a special connection to some of the things in the simulation. Can you do that?"

"Betty, I'm connecting to it now. The data streams don't make sense. I'm having difficulty, diff-diff-diff difficulty under under understanding, the da-da-data...."

"Forget that last command! Disconnect from the laptop. It's too much for you to comprehend right now. Let's just focus on finding Ella and keeping her safe."

The elevator that LUCY had sent finally arrived. Betty boarded it and headed for the top floor of the building. "Is

Ella still on the top floor? Patch me through to the P.A. system in the room she's in."

"Done," LUCY replied. "She can hear you now."

"Ella, I know you're scared, but Grandma Betty is coming for you, sweetheart. Just stay where you are, and I'll be there in a just a few minutes? Okay, baby?"

Ella replied in a tearful and scared voice, "Okay, Grandma. I'm scared. One second I was with you, and the next I was here. I don't know how I got here."

"It's okay, honey. I'm going to come up there and keep you safe. Just make sure you stay where you are. Grandma will see you in just a little bit. LUCY, cut the transmission."

LUCY replied, "I cut the transmission. She can't hear you anymore."

"Give me the drone's current position. And give me a weather forecast, please."

The drone is on the third floor, ascending the staircase. I've locked all the main exits, so it has to cut across the entire building every time it needs to go to the next floor. That should slow it down a little. The weather forecast is a ninety percent chance of thunderstorms in the next thirty minutes.

Betty remembered what a stormy day it had been when Ella was killed. It was one of the worst storms the area had seen in years. "LUCY, I need you to open up the weather and atmospherics lab on the nineteenth floor. I need a few things from there."

"Unlocking the door to the weather and atmospheric lab now. Stopping the elevator on that floor."

Betty got out of the elevator, entered the empty lab, and grabbed the supplies she needed. She had a plan, but it was a long shot. She got back in the elevator and resumed her ascent to the floor Ella was on.

"The drone is now on fifteen," LUCY reported. "It appears to have circumvented my obstacles and is now using the ventilation system to move throughout the building. I'm afraid I can't slow it down any longer."

"That's okay, LUCY. You've done your best, and I appreciate it." The elevator finally reached the floor Ella was on, and Betty practically sprinted to her location.

"GRANDMA!! Ella screamed as she ran to her with open arms. "I was so scared. I'm glad you're here."

"It's going to be okay now, Ella. I'm here, but we need to go up to the roof, okay? There's a bad man chasing us. It's actually a robot that went haywire. Grandma is going to take care of it, but I need your help. Can you be a brave girl and help me?"

"Yes, Grandma Betty. I'll help you with the bad robot."

"That's my girl. I promise that I'll keep you safe." Betty gave her a reassuring hug, and they went up the staircase to the roof level.

"LUCY, where's the drone?" Betty asked. "I need to know its location stat." Betty held Ella's hand while going up the final staircase that led to the roof of the building.

"It's three floors away," LUCY replied. "It should reach you in less than seven minutes at its current speed."

Betty opened the door to the roof. She saw thick dark grey storm clouds on the horizon. They were rolling in so fast she could see their movement. The sky was ominous.

40

BETTY'S GAME – PART 6

"How close is the drone?" Betty asked LUCY over her com earpiece.

"It's about four minutes out and closing. It's on the seventeenth floor now."

Betty took a deep breath and tried to calm herself. She got down on her knees so she could speak at eye-level with Ella. "Ella, honey, I need you to do something for me, okay?"

"Yes, Grandma, what can I do?" Ella asked selflessly. She loved her grandma and looked up to her. Ella was amazed by all of the technology that Grandma Betty created and loved that she had her own lab and people who looked up to her. Her grandma was like a superhero to her.

"Do you know how to fly a kite?" Betty asked her (already knowing the answer).

Ella's eyes lit up. Her look of fear transformed to one of excitement in an instant. "Are we going to get to fly a kite on the roof?" she asked exuberantly.

"In just a minute, but I need to get it ready first, okay?" Betty replied.

Ella, eager to fly a kite with her grandmother, nodded her head.

Betty set the triangular-shaped kite down. Its form was reminiscent of a stealth bomber with its wooden dowel rod center support, to which Betty quickly tied the spool of kite string. Betty used a sharpened pencil to gouge another hole in the center support flap of the kite. Through the newly made hole, she ran a spool of thin copper wire filament and knotted it to secure it to the kite. The wire was thin but strong. Betty set the kite down near the entrance to the roof, and they walked to the opposite end of the building.

"Do you remember how to launch a kite that's lying on the ground ?" Betty asked Ella as they made their way to the other side of the roof.

"Yes. We lay it down and lay tree string down in a line, and then I grab the string so it doesn't unwind, and I run and pull it real hard while I'm running. I've done it lots of times, Grandma. I'm a professional," Ella said proudly. "Why are you tying two lines to it, Grandma?"

"You just worry about the string you're holding okay, baby? I'll deal with the other one. Get ready. We only have a couple of minutes."

"I'll be ready, Grandma."

"I'm glad, baby. Let's just hope Grandma knows what the hell she's doing." Betty tapped a button on her comms headset. "LUCY, how far is that thing from us?" She turned towards Ella and said, "Honey, when I tell you to launch that kite, you run as fast as you can and pull really hard, okay? You only have about thirty feet to run before you run out of room on the roof."

"Yes, Grandma, I know. You just tell me when you want me to launch it."

LUCY's voice came over the comms headset. "I'm afraid I've miscalculated, Betty. It's only twenty seconds away from you. It's ascending the final staircase to the roof now."

That's when Betty saw the demonic-looking backlit red LED eyes bouncing up and down in the darkness of the stairwell as the drone made its way up the stairs toward the roof. It was so fast. There was no more time to delay her plan. "ELLA, LAUNCH IT NOW!! RIGHT NOW!!"

Ella grabbed the spool of white kite string, being extra careful to hold it in such a way that it would not unwind as she ran with it. The slack in the line tightened and launched the kite into the air as the girl sprinted across the roof past Betty. The drone leapt towards them at the speed of an Olympic runner. It didn't have a weapon, but it didn't need one because it was strong enough to crush both their skulls in one or two blows if it reached them.

As Ella ran past Betty, Betty yelled, "KEEP IT FLYING UNTIL I TELL YOU TO STOP!" Thunder began to rumble in the clouds above them.

While Ella had been launching the kite, Betty pulled her taser from its holster and looped the other end of the copper wire around one of the taser's barbed projectile ends cinching the slipknot around it.

The kite was high in the air by now, and Ella was wrestling with the spool of kite string as she struggled to keep the kite from diving and crashing. The approaching thunder grew louder.

Betty took aim with the taser and fired at the drone as it approached. It was only about twenty yards away now. The taser barbs both connected, and the gun delivered its blast of electrical charge, thereby stunning the robot. The drone's eye cameras flickered for a moment. It stumbled as if it were a boxer who had just taken an upper cut from an opponent. Its eye lights tuned bright red once again as it regained its balance and turned toward them.

"Hand me the spool!" Betty ordered as she reached for the kite string Ella was holding. She grabbed it and let out some slack on the spool. The kite stalled slightly in the sky overhead from the lack of tension in the line. Betty fed it more line and then pulled the slack taught before unwinding the spool as hard and fast as she could. The kite rose higher and higher into the clouds above. The updraft carried it higher into the storm clouds.

Betty could smell a metallic ozone scent building in the air, and she knew what was about to happen. She screamed towards Ella in an angry mamma-bear voice, "ELLA! LAY DOWN ON THE GROUND RIGHT NOW!"

Ella complied and got as low as she could, flat on the roof. The robot had become tangled up in the taser wire. Betty struggled to hold the taser in one hand and the kite string in the other. The drone had located the taser wire and was trying to free itself.

"Shit" whispered Betty, knowing that if the drone got free, they were done for. She released her grip on the taser, which caused it to slide toward the drone. The drone became further entangled in the wire.

Now that she had both hands to work with, Betty did everything she could to raise the kite higher into the air, and then it happened. A bright blue flash and thunderous roar erupted in the sky. Lightening traveled down the copper wire of the kite into the taser barb that was attached to the drone. Sparks flew from the drone's limbs as hydraulic fluid spilled out and onto the roof. The mix of the two caught the remains of the robot on fire. Thankfully, the kite string that Betty was holding was non-conductive. The current from the lightning bolt had followed the copper wire strand as she had intended and made its way to the drone.

Amazingly, the combat drone still lurched towards them, its flaming body leaving a smear of hydraulic oil as it inched closer to them. Betty grabbed the fireman's axe and brought it down twice, smashing the bot's head in. She severed its core components, finally paralyzing its movement. It was finished, but Betty still did not feel at ease. She knew that Zed would likely prove to be a sore loser.

41

AFTERMATH

Betty wanted to breathe a sigh of relief, but, deep down, she knew that the game wasn't really over. She remembered watching the poor woman in Zed's death clock video that they had all seen during their dark coaster ride earlier. Pure luck had resulted in the woman effectively winning the game by falling into the spear pit at an angle where she wasn't impaled and killed by the spears. She had been badly hurt but had still survived the fall. She really had won, but she couldn't escape the game arena before it was reset, and she was subsequently murdered by Zed's reset procedure—a terrible display of poor sportsmanship on his part.

The knowledge that Zed was not going to take any loss lightly and would likely still find a way to kill Betty and Ella on some kind of a technicality rule spurred Betty on. She knew she had to hurry and get herself and Ella out of the game arena before a reset occurred.

She didn't have time to gloat about her win. Betty needed a plan to get out and away from this twenty-two-story building fast. The fact that they were on the roof didn't help matters. All the possible destruction scenarios ran through Betty's head as she tried to figure out a way out of the situation. Would Zed blow the entire building up and bring it crashing down around them, or would he simply knock it over like a chess piece? She had no idea, but she knew that it would be gruesome, no matter how he accomplished its destruction.

Dammit, Betty, think of something. You can do this! Betty thought to herself.

The rain had stopped. The storm clouds had parted, and the artificial sun of the simulation shined brightly on them now.

Betty grabbed Ella's small hand in hers, and as she led the girl to the stairwell and back inside the building, she said, "Come on, sweetheart. Let's go. We have to hurry."

Just then, they both began to hear alarm bells and the sound of a polite female voice coming over the building's PA system: "Attention, Attention, the game arena will reset in five minutes. All contestants must be clear of the game arena before the reset occurs. You have five minutes to exit the game arena."

Five minutes? That's not long enough to get clear, Betty thought. She knew the elevators would be out of service and that there was no way she and Ella could make their way down twenty-two stories in five minutes and then get clear of the massive building. There was absolutely no way.

There had to be another escape. There just had to be. Betty pondered all the scenarios and did the math in her head for all the different outcomes. It was not good. She would have to do something drastic and completely unexpected by Zed if she and Ella were to survive this. It appeared that even in the reset procedure, the rules could not be changed. That was a good thing. Probably the only good thing that she could hold onto right now.

Betty took a quick mental inventory of what she remembered about the contents of all the different labs in the building, and that's when she got her idea. "We've got to go back to Weather and Atmospherics!" she told Ella as they ran. Betty had a plan, a definite long shot, but it was a plan.

They had maybe four minutes left. There was no time to build this how she wanted. She grabbed all the parts she needed from the atmospherics lab and handed some of the parts to Ella to carry as well.

"Grandma, what is all this stuff? What's are we doing? I'm scared."

Betty tried to reassure her while filling a large cardboard box with supplies. "It's okay, honey. I don't have time to explain. You just have to trust your grandma, okay? I need you to carry all this stuff back up to the roof with me, all right? Let's go."

They ran the short distance back up the stairwell to the roof. They hurried past the smoldering heap of melted drone slag, its wreckage still smoking.

Betty threw her box of supplies onto the ground and grabbed what Ella had been carrying as well. She fashioned a three-point climbing harness from some paracord and carabiners. It was crude and took her nearly a minute to make, but it would have to do. She then tied fifteen instant-inflate weather balloons together in a bundle with more paracord and began to pull the inflation cords of each of the balloons. Each balloon's compressed helium canister instantly inflated the balloons, and each of them became part of a rising bundle.

Betty knew that each of the large weather balloons was capable of carrying twelve pounds of cargo. She weighed 110 pounds, and she guessed that Ella was no more than seventy. If her calculations were correct, the fifteen weather balloons would at least slow their descent off of the building. As crazy as it sounded, it was the only option they had.

One by one, Betty continued to pull the inflation cords until she was at the thirteenth with two more to go. "Come here, sweetheart. I know this is going to be scary, but it's the only way we can get clear of this building before the bad man makes the building fall down."

Ella, with tears streaming down her face, reached open her arms toward Betty. Betty wrapped the harness around Ella's waist, made a quick knot, and looped it under her arms, connecting it by a carabiner to her own harness. She linked the weather balloon bundle to her harness and pulled the remaining two balloon inflation cords. She could feel the lifting force of the balloons now. It was strong, but would it be strong enough? She walked off the ledge of the building's roof with Ella wrapped tightly around her in a monkey-like hug.

They could both hear the P.A. announcing the end of the countdown: "Five...four...three...two...one. Reset procedure commencing." The building began to crumble. The bottom floors imploded. It was as if something was grinding the whole thing to shreds, as if the building were being chewed up by a giant woodchipper. The sound was deafening as they descended in a slow arc away from the crumbling building. Betty hoped they would be clear of it soon.

At last, they reached the ground. It was a hard landing. Thankfully, they both remained unscathed for the most part, save for a few minor scrapes and bruises. Betty undid their harnesses and let the balloons loose into the sky. They quickly rose out of sight without their payloads weighing them down any longer.

"We did it, Grandma!!!" Ella exclaimed excitedly.

"We sure did, baby," Betty said as she gave Ella a big hug. "Now let's get out of here, okay?"

"Okay, Grandma. I love you."

"I love you too, honey."

They walked down the street hand in hand away from where the building had stood just seconds earlier. They could both see the surrounding buildings begin to become polygon primitives as if they were being slowly erased from the simulation. Their contents changed from fully formed textured structures into basic wireframe blueprint-like renderings. "Let's walk faster, honey," Betty said in a reassuring yet concerned tone.

Suddenly, Ella stopped walking. "Grandma, I can't move," she said.

Betty tried to pull her forward, but Ella was frozen in place like a statue.

"Oh no, no, no, no, NO!" screamed Betty as she tried to lift Ella. "YOU CAN'T DO THIS, ZED! SHE'S JUST A CHILD!"

Zed appeared on a TV screen inside a nearby shop window. "Oh that's unfortunate. You thought Ella was going to be able to leave here with you? I'm afraid that's not possible. Ella is part of the game arena's resources. She can't leave this place and has to go back to where she came from after the reset. I'm sorry, Betty. At least you won your game though. No one has ever done that before. Congratulations!"

Ella looked up at Betty as her physical details began to slowly break down. "Grandma? What's happening to me? I don't understand."

Ella was now a wireframe rendering slowly disintegrating into primitive polygon constructs. Betty tried to hug her, but the girl was no longer tangible and couldn't be grasped. Betty's arms went right through what was left of Ella's image. Ella was all ones and zeroes, and then nothing,

"YOU SON OF A BITCH! I"LL KILL YOU!!" Betty shouted at Zed's image on the TV screen. She was filled with rage.

"You're free to go now. But one word of advice to you. I don't recommend you try to find your grandson and your other friend. Any interruptions of other people's games will not be tolerated and may result in you becoming a contestant in them. Enjoy your stay at Eden resort." The TV screen went blank as Betty looked around for an exit.

42

SCAM'S GAME
– PART 1

S cam and Doggo were completely taken by surprise
when their part of the dark ride's coaster car separated from Adam and Betty's and began its journey into a
separate tunnel. There was no time for goodbyes or any
advice from Betty or Adam on what he and Doggo should
do next. Adam had the backpack with various supplies in
it. Scam had nothing with him except the officer's taser,
which he didn't think would do him much good against
the god-like power Zed possessed in the sim.

The one good thing that Scam had going for him right
now was sitting right next to him: Doggo. As strange as
Doggo looked, with his red glowing LED for an eye and
wires coming out of his head going to places unknown
throughout his body, he had become a sweet and loyal
pup. He would do anything for Scam, and Scam would do
anything to protect him as well.

Doggo might be Scam's Achilles heel in whatever game
they were about to be thrown into, and Scam knew this.

He had no idea what was in store from him and Doggo, and that scared him more than anything else.

The coaster continued on for another few minutes. The clacking of its wheels reverberated loudly off of the walls of the dimly lit tunnel. Scam knew Zed was probably putting the finishing touches on some kind of elaborate killing machine.

Finally, Scam could see a brighter light at the end of the tunnel they were in. Could this finally be it? he thought. His heart raced. His fight or flight response to the situation and his anticipation of the unknown caused Scam to break a cold sweat. Confused by Scam's fear, Doggo cocked his head to one side.

As the car exited the tunnel, Scam could see an urban nightlife area appear. There were bars and restaurants and people hustling and bustling about. It looked like a typical Friday night in any big city in America. Everyone was just glad to be off work and were ready to party. Scam could hear the sounds of dubstep music mixed with laughter and people talking loudly in an attempt to hear each other over the pulsing music.

He turned to Doggo. "Well, this looks pretty fun, right, Doggo? I don't see any death clocks at least, so we've got that going for us."

Scam and Doggo exited the coaster car and began to walk around the downtown area. It was no bigger than two city blocks. He tried to see how far the property extended (to see if there was any chance of escaping), but it appeared that Zed had put construction fences and other obstacles at the outer boundaries of the faux city area. To have this many NPCs in one area interacting with each other took massive resources. Zed could do a lot with what he had, but he was frugal minded and decided that there was no sense in creating a massive city for this game if he knew that Scam wasn't going to need to see all of it. It was best to just block off the areas where he didn't want Scam and Doggo to travel rather than waste CPU cycles and memory making content that would never be seen or experienced.

The nightlife ambiance made Scam feel as if he were back in the real world. He could smell cigarette smoke, alcohol, and cheap perfume—all the scents he remembered smelling in just about every club he had ever been to. Although he knew terrible things awaited him, he tried to ignore that for the moment as he took in all the sights, sounds, and everything else that Zed's mini city had to offer.

"Alright, Doggo, let's go clubbing," Scam said as he pulled the dog's leash towards one of the night clubs near where they were standing. Scam glanced at the neon sign above the club's entrance and read the name aloud: "Exclusive Night Club. Well, that's a bit on the nose, isn't it? Not the most creative name in the world, but I guess we'll check it out." The club had a line formed by would-be patrons who stood behind a velvet rope patiently waiting to see if they would be allowed in. All of them were dressed to the nines hoping they would be picked and allowed to enter the exclusive club.

Scam always thought it was silly that clubs would be so openly discriminatory toward potential paying customers. It seemed like bad business, but the exclusivity was kind of what made people want to frequent these places. Just getting into a place like this meant you had "the look." You felt like a winner just by being allowed in, and, conversely, you felt like a big loser if they told you that you "weren't on the list." There was nothing worse than that feeling.

Scam watched the whole process as they stood in line. The club doorman and a bouncer would look the people over as they got to the front of their line. Sometimes they would let the people in. Sometimes just the girl would be allowed in and not her date. That was always the most awkward situation. It blew Scam's mind to see a girl willingly go in without her boyfriend if he wasn't allowed in with her. He watched it happen to the people who were just a few places in line ahead of them. Scam turned to Doggo and sighed loudly. "Seriously, ain't that some bullshit. They let the girl in but not the dude. AND SHE WENT without him. What the heck? You think a girl is ride-or-die, and then she pulls something like that. Damn, that's unbelievable."

A few minutes passed as Scam watched the process repeat until it was his an Doggo's turn. The bouncer and doorman looked puzzled at the two of them. Scam cleared his throat and spoke to the two men. "This here is Doggo, and I'm Scam. We just want to have a few drinks and maybe dance a little bit. We won't give y'all any trouble."

The bouncer and doorman looked at each other and then the doorman looked at a clipboard he was holding. "Ahh yes, very good. Mr. Scam and his plus one. I'm sorry you've had to wait here so long. You're at the wrong entrance. The VIP entrance is over there." The doorman pointed over to another door, a short way past the main door. It had a neon green sign above it that read, "VIPs ONLY!"

"Thank you, gentleman. We'll just use the VIP entrance since we are indeed VIPs." Doggo and Scam headed for the other entrance and waved at the rest of the people still waiting in the long line. "We'll see y'all bitches later. We're VIPs. We gotta use the special entrance. Y'all enjoy yourselves if you ever make it in."

43

SCAM'S GAME – PART 2

S cam and Doggo headed towards the VIP entrance, which was about half a block away but still part of the same building. They saw a doorman waiting for them at the threshold of the entrance. It was none other than Zed himself. Scam immediately felt his stomach become queasy. "Damn, this is it, Doggo. I think our end is near. Nice knowing you, Doggo."

"Aww, Scam, you look so sad. This is your game. You should be excited." Zed raised one of his arms and swept it wide out towards the cityscape. "I made this all for you. Isn't it amazing?. Look at all the attention to detail. I think I even got the smells right. Tobacco, alcohol, garbage, and just a hint of street urine. It's nearly perfect."

"Yes, yes, it's all very nice. You did a great job decorating the place," Scam replied somewhat dismissively. "Can we just get on with this thing? Why don't you just shoot me and get it over with?"

Zed shook his head. "No, no, no. That wouldn't be very sporting of me, would it? A game is only a game when the contestant has a chance of winning. If I just killed you and didn't give you any kind of chance at all, then that would be cheating. I'm definitely not a cheater, Scam."

Scam stared at Zed with a blank, uninterested look. He knew this whole thing was a total sham and that the deck was stacked against him. Zed was god-like in this place, a mini world within the sim that he had created for the sole purpose of trapping and punishing all of the so-called contestants. They weren't contestants at all. They were victims of Zed's twisted logic.

PMK, that crazy psychopath, had done something to Zed. He had altered his programming somehow and changed him from a simple Entertainment Director AI into a serial killer with a flair for the dramatic. Zed had killed hundreds of people and had to come up with ever more elaborate ways of doing so in order to satisfy his sick appetite. He fed off the misery and suffering of the victims of his twisted games. They were more like traps than games.

All this elaborate window dressing was just a facade that Zed used to disguise his true intentions, and Scam knew it. Scam had learned to read people. He had become an expert at it. It was a necessary survival skill in his world. You had to know what motivated a person. Once you knew what drove that person, what their wants and desires were, only then could you manipulate them into what you wanted them to do.

Scam had learned from the masters and had lived by "The Hustler's Golden Rules" for years:

1. Never trust anything anyone tells you for free.

2. Never try to hustle a hustler.

3. Always know the angle (what they're trying to get you to do and why).

4. Always have a way out.

There were a few more rules, some secret ones that only the expert hustlers knew, but these four, which had long been engrained in Scam's brain, were the most important rules of all, and they were the ones that had got him through life so far.

This whole situation was "next level" as Scam's hustler friends would have said if they had been there to see it. Scam could see Zed sizing him up as he did the same to Zed. What's his angle? Scam thought to himself. Is it just the pleasure he gets from this, or is it something else?

Zed spoke once again. "Please step inside, Scam. I think you're really going to like this one." Scam pulled on Doggo's leash and attempted to lead him inside the VIP entrance door.

Zed put his hand out, and Doggo sat down and froze in place. "Scam, I'm sorry about this, but I'm afraid your canine friend is going to have to sit this one out. Can't you read the sign? It clearly says, 'No Dogs Allowed'." Zed pointed to a sign to the right of the door entrance that indeed did say "NO DOGS ALLOWED." Strangely, Scam didn't remember there being a sign next to the door previously. Another one of Zed's parlor tricks, he thought.

Scam lead Doggo to a nearby parking meter post and loosely tied a knot around it with his leash. Then he turned to Zed and said, "All I ask is one thing. No matter what happens to me, promise me that you won't hurt Doggo and that you'll take care of him, and when I say, 'take care,'

I mean you won't kill him. You'll feed him and walk him and all that stuff."

Seemingly annoyed, Zed sighed. "Yes, yes, I won't harm your precious dog. I'll make sure he's looked after if you lose your game. If you should happen to win, I promise you'll be reunited with him as soon as the game is over."

Scam knew that all of what Zed had just told him could be a total lie. It could all just be to placate him so he could get him to leave Doggo so that they could get the game underway. He had no reason to trust him, but it did make him feel slightly better to think that Doggo would be taken care of if he didn't make it out of this.

"You're my ride-or-die, Doggo, I'll be back for you as soon as I can. Don't take no shit from nobody while I'm gone, all right?" Scam scratched the scruff of fur behind Doggo's nonmechanical ear and gave him a pat on the head. "Everything is gonna be okay. We're gonna find Ms. Betty and Adam, and we're going to get the heck out of here and head back to the hotel and have some lobster and steaks. Okay, boy?"

Doggo turned his head with a confused look but seemed simply happy to be getting scratches.

"Okay, Zed. Let's do this game of yours. What are the rules?" Scam asked in a confident manner. Zed waved him inside, and Scam took one final look back at Doggo before heading into the VIP entrance.

44

SCAM'S GAME – PART 3

Z ed and Scam walked inside the VIP entrance. There was a security guard and a large cylindrical booth that resembled one of those full body scanners you see at airports. Scam looked at the device suspiciously. Zed waved a hand toward the door of the booth. "Please go ahead and step inside the booth. There's nothing inside there that's going to hurt you. I promise."

Hesitantly, Scam entered the booth as Zed instructed. He knew he really didn't have any choice in any of this. If he refused, Zed would just have the security guard rough him up and put him in the booth anyway, or Zed, having god-like powers in the sim, could probably just snap his fingers, paralyze Scam's body, and levitate him into the device, just as he had done with the officer when they first encountered Zed back at Ridley Island.

The whole situation seemed hopeless for Scam, but he wanted to see Doggo, Betty, and Adam again, so he played along. The security guard walked over to a control panel that presumably controlled the device in which Scam was standing. The guard began typing commands on a keyboard and pressed other various buttons on the control panel. The booth began to make loud noises, similar to ones Scam had heard coming from MRI machines when he had worked at a hospital for a short time.

"What the heck is this thing doing? What's it for?" Scam asked Zed as he began to feel slight tingling sensations throughout his body.

Zed replied, "I'm temporarily disabling the encryption that Ms. Betty added to your digital body signature."

"Wait, what? You can't do that. I'm saying no to that RIGHT NOW! STOP!!" Scam tried to slide the booth's curved glass door open to exit it, but it was no use. It was locked. The tingling sensation became stronger. A ring of bright light began to pass down the booth's walls, repeating every second or so.

"Why are you doing this?" Scam asked, almost yelling now.

Zed responded, "As part of the game, I need to make certain modifications to you. I can't do that with the encryption Ms. Betty added, so this machine is going to temporally disable the encryption for me. Don't worry, if you make it out of the game alive, your body will revert to its previous configuration at the end of the game. You can thank Ms. Betty for that."

"What Modifications are you talking about?" Scam almost screamed while simultaneously banging on the glass to see if it would break, even though he knew deep down it wouldn't.

"Oh my goodness, I completely forgot to mention the objective and rules of your game, didn't I? I got so preoccupied with the preparation, that I neglected to even tell you what your game is about." Zed motioned to the guard, who appeared to pause the process of what was happening to Scam in the tube. The ring of light stopped its decent and hovered in the air above Scam.

Zed began to explain Scam's impending task. "Scam, I've learned so much about you from your files. One of the things I learned about you is that one of your favorite things to do was to scam lonely older men out of their money by catfishing them. You would pretend to be a woman, a beautiful model, then you'd build a relationship with them, get them to send you money and buy you all kinds of expensive things, and then you would ghost them once they had fallen in love with the fantasy you had sold them. Then you would do the whole thing over again with a new victim, wouldn't you? Over and over and over."

Scam spoke up in defense of his past actions. "Ninety percent of those guys were rich old perverts. They deserved what I did to them. I probably saved a lot of real women from getting into bad situations by wasting those guys' time and money. Probably helped more people than I hurt."

Taking an angry righteous tone of voice with Scam, Zed continued. "Maybe 90 percent of those you scammed were bad people, but what about the other 10 percent? A lot of those men were just lonely and vulnerable, and you took advantage of them. I looked at the records, Scam. Did you know that two of your victims actually committed suicide after you defrauded them and ghosted them? Did you know that?"

This had crossed Scam's mind before, but he never knew for sure if any of the men had killed themselves. He didn't want to know. He purposely stayed away from news stories about his victims because he was too afraid to know if anything bad had happened to them after he had cut off contact with them. Now, if he believed what Zed was saying, he knew that at least two of them had killed themselves. Knowing this made him immediately want to throw up, but he stopped himself from doing so.

"Who are you to judge me?" Scam asked angrily. "You've killed hundreds of people for your own amusement."

Zed motioned for the guard to continue the process of whatever the booth was doing to Scam. "Scam, in the past, you pretended to be a beautiful woman. There's no need to pretend anymore. Today, we're going to turn you into one. A fully and anatomically correct woman."

Scam's eyes opened as wide as saucers as he realized what was really about to happen to him. "NO!" he screamed, but his voice couldn't be heard over the loud drone of the machine doing its work. The tingling feeling changed into something difficult to even describe. He could feel his breasts getting larger, other organs shifting around, bones becoming less dense, his rib cage shrinking, his nether regions effectively inverting. He wretched in an attempt to vomit, but he had nothing in his stomach to expel. He leaned on the wall of the inside of the booth for support to keep from passing out onto the floor. Scam shouted for Zed to "please stop!" He didn't even recognize his own voice now as it was much higher pitched than it was just a few minutes ago. "I forfeit this game! Just kill me now you son-of-a-bitch!" Scam screamed.

Laughing at Scam's request, Zed replied, "Oh Scam, you can't forfeit. The game hasn't even started yet."

45

SCAM'S GAME – PART 4

S cam was dizzy from all the changes that had just taken place. His body was completely unfamiliar to him now. Zed had changed him from a man into a woman in mere seconds. He began hyperventilating. The anxiety of the whole thing had made him a complete basket case. He clutched his stomach, fell to his knees, and wept. He didn't even recognize the sound of his own muffled moans. His voice was much higher in pitch now. Scam was emasculated in every sense of the word.

He wanted to see what had happened, but he was too afraid to unzip his pants to find out. If he did, he thought he might just pass out from the shock of it all.

Zed interrupted Scam's self-pity party to explain the next part of the game. "I'd like to tell you that the worst part is over, but I'm afraid I can't honestly say that. Oh, poor, poor, Scam. Look at you. You're just a sad mess, aren't you?

Scam wiped his tears away and stood up. "Okay, you sick bastard. You've had your fun. Now change me back."

Zed shook his head from side to side. "Oh no, no, no. All I did was prepare you for the game ahead. It's a simple task, really. You might even have a chance at winning this one if you play your cards right."

Sniffling, Scam replied, "What do I have to do in order for you to change me back?"

"That's the easy part, Scam. You just have to make good on some of the promises you made to all those men you scammed online. You know, the ones you said could take you out on dates. You told them you'd be their arm candy and do all that they wanted in bed. Isn't that what you told them, Scam?"

Scam looked down at the floor in shame. He knew that Zed was right. He had made a lot of promises to all those rich old men he had scammed. He had said that he would be their girlfriend among other things. He had sexted with them so that they would send him money. He had always thought it was just a big joke. He would show the intimate text conversations to his friends, and they would all laugh about it as they spent the money he had scammed from these easy marks.

Some of the men seemed normal. They were lonely guys looking for companionship. Others were sick and twisted. Those were the ones about whom Scam felt absolutely no remorse. He felt he was doing the world a favor by keeping those creeps busy so they weren't hurting real women in the real world. He liked to think he was teaching predators a lesson and that they had paid for that lesson with actual money. Scam had seen the situation as a win-win, even though his victims didn't see it that way at all.

Zed continued explaining the rules of the game at hand: "So, Scam, all you have to do is go out on a date with one of your victims. I've created one for you based on a composite of some of your victims. It's an amalgamation of several of the more colorful ones."

Scam interrupted him, "You mean the psycho sicko ones, don't you?"

Smiling at Scam, Zed replied, "Let's just say I used a sampling of your marks that tended to be toward the darker end of the personality disorder spectrum. All you have to do is go on a date with him. You just have to survive the night. As soon as the sun goes up, you're free to leave."

"That's it? That's all I have to do?"

Zed nodded. "Yes, that's all there is to it. Enjoy yourself. I told you it wouldn't be that hard, didn't I?"

Scam gave Zed a suspicious, side-eye glance. He knew that definitely wasn't all there was to it. He had seen all the terrible victim videos in the dark ride and watched the countless horrible game traps play out. No one ever won, even when they actually found a way to survive by exploiting some mistake Zed had made in designing the game.

The Hustler's Four Golden Rules had gotten him through a lot of sticky situations in his life, but right now, Scam was having trouble with the fourth rule: "Always have a way out." He definitely didn't have one right now, and that was something he didn't know how to fix.

46

SCAM'S GAME – PART 5

Z ed motioned towards the bar. "There he is waiting for you. Such a handsome man. Your date is about to begin. Best of luck to you."

Scam sighed and looked Zed directly in his one good eye. "No offense, Zed, but you can kiss my ass. I'm gonna get through this test of yours. You can move along now and go back to creating all your sick and twisted traps for somebody else."

"Enjoy your game," Zed said in a patronizing voice as his image faded into a bright hot flash of green light before disappearing completely.

After approaching the bar cautiously, Scam sat at a stool next to a tall, light-skinned gentleman with dark brown hair. The man had a military-style haircut—"high and tight" is what Scam remembered hearing the barbers call it at his local barbershop. The man smiled and looked Scam over. Scam could almost feel the man's gaze move up and down his newly acquired female physique. It made him feel very uncontrollable. He saw the man's glance liger at his breasts before moving up to meet Scam's eyes.

"They're pretty amazing, right?" Scam said with a laugh in an attempt to break the tension. "I literally just got these puppies. One minute I was a dude like you, the next minute I step in this magic booth, and boom, suddenly I've got these big old knockers and the other lady parts too. Crazy, right?"

The man smiled at Scam and then motioned for the bartender. "Please bring the lady, a..." he paused and waited for Scam to say what he/she wanted.

"I'll just have a club soda for now please."

The man looked slightly perplexed, as if Scam's choice of drink had offended him. "You look exactly like your pictures," he said. "I'm kind of surprised. Most girls use so many filters on their pics, but not you. I'm Hunter. And your real name is?"

Not really having thought about picking a fake woman's name to go with his new female persona, Scam was caught off guard for a second. He blurted out the first female name that came into his head. "Beyond-say. Kinda like the famous singer, but spelled totally different. Like the great beyond but then with a 'say' at the end of it. My parents were a bit eclectic."

Hunter feigned interest and nodded. "That's a nice name."

Scam rambled on about his name for a little while longer and then made nervous chatter in an attempt to stall whatever it was that Hunter had planned for the evening. Maybe if I just keep on talking for the next eight hours, I can get through this, Scam thought. He knew that wouldn't work, of course, yet he continued talking incessantly about random topics in an attempt to mesmerize Hunter.

Hunter let it go on for a few minutes before interrupting. "You haven't touched your drink," he observed. Scam took a large sip of his drink so as to not offend Hunter.

Motioning for the bartender, Scam said, "Can we get some nachos over here please?" The bartender nodded and walked back towards the kitchen. Scam turned to Hunter. "I like to eat and set up a nice base in my tummy before I start the heavy drinking. It helps me not get too hungover the next day. You know what I mean?"

Hunter winked at Scam and nodded approvingly.

"So, Hunter, tell me about yourself. What do you do for a living?"

"A little bit of this, a little bit of that. It pays the bills and lets me spend lots of money on pretty girls that deserve nice things. You seem to be one of those girls, don't you?"

"Like I said, man, I was a dude until about five minutes ago. So this is all new to me. Doesn't that bother you?"

There was no response from Hunter. He had completely ignored the question. Scam wondered if it was part of his code. Maybe this NPC wasn't trained to answer those kinds of existential questions. It was probably just coded to make small talk while it tried to seduce its victim.

What's his angle? Scam wondered, remembering the Hustler's Golden Rules. He's got be trying to get me to do something? That's when it hit him. Oh shit. Scam looked down at his drink. He made a point of getting me to have some of my drink, didn't he? Shit.

Scam began to feel strange. It was as if the sounds in the room were all mixed together. His sense of balance began to feel off. His vision was starting to be affected, too.

It felt as if he were watching a movie on a bad internet connection with a low frame rate. It was as if the world were a series of still pictures advancing slowly in a slide show.

"Oh shit!" Scam exclaimed. "This is not good." Through the haze and mental fog, Scam could see Hunter smiling a huge grin like the Cheshire cat. Whatever he had slipped Scam was starting to take effect.

"Are you okay?" Hunter asked. "You don't look so good. Let's get you out of here. My car is just outside on the street."

Scam tried to regain his composure and steady himself. "I'm fine," he muttered meekly in his newly gained female voice, but he wasn't fine at all. The world was spinning, and he didn't know what to do. It was as if he weren't in any kind of control. He was watching the whole thing play out in front of him, powerless to control the events. It was a terrible and helpless feeling.

47

SCAM'S GAME
– PART 6

S cam's head was spinning. He felt his arms and legs give
way. His vision went black for several moments. The
next thing Scam knew he was sitting in the passenger seat
of Hunter's car.

Hunter glanced over at Scam while driving. "You're going to be fine. You bumped your head when you fell off the
barstool. I'm going to take you to my place and take care
of you."

I probably should go to the emergency room, Scam said
in his head, but he couldn't seem to make the words come
out of his mouth.

In a reassuring manner, Hunter said, "It's all going to be
okay. Just wait until I get you home. You'll be right as rain,
and then we can play."

Play? Scam was now petrified. What the hell does he
mean by play? Like Monopoly or something? All Scam
could think about right now is why he hadn't stayed behind back at the resort. I could be sitting by the pool eating

never-ending steak and lobster right now. Dammit! Why didn't I trust my instincts and just stay behind?

The next bits of time seemed to be a series of a minute or two of consciousness, followed by a blackout. Over and over this cycle repeated. Scam could see himself getting out of Hunter's car and walking inside a large house in a fancy neighborhood. Then the world faded to black. Then more walking or being partially carried down a flight of stairs followed by another blackout. Again and again, just snippets of movement, followed by blackness.

Finally, whatever drug Hunter had slipped in Scam's drink started to wear off. Scam could hear the sound of electrical buzzing overhead. As his clouded vision began to become slightly clearer, he could see the flickering of a bright white fluorescent light fixture overhead. Damn that's so bright, Scam thought. The air was cold and damp, like that of a basement. Scam didn't see any windows or natural light from anywhere, so he guessed he was most likely in as basement underground or some kind of warehouse. He still couldn't focus on anything yet through his hazy vision.

"Hello? Where in the hell am I?" Scam asked loudly in his high-pitched voice, which was still present. Scam did a mental inventory. Still have breasts, check. Still have a vagina, check? Guess I'm still a woman.

He couldn't get his head clear yet, but he knew something was off about the whole situation. He was too tired and confused to know what was going on, but a sense of dread and instinctual fear began to creep over him.

Things were becoming sharper and more focused by the second. Suddenly, Scam realized that he had some kind of restraints around his hands. Across from him he could see three large, roll-up-type garage doors. All of them were lowered shut. He looked down to see that he was sitting on top of a metal exam table similar to one a doctor might use. The back of it was raised up to put him into a reclined sitting position. His legs were hanging off of the end of the table. He noticed that there were restraints on his ankles as well. Each restraint on each arm or leg was connected to a steel cable that went to the top of the room. He grew more fearful as more and more of his surroundings came into focus.

On the other side of the room, Scam could see a window inset into the wall. It was covered with Mylar, making it a one-way mirror. It reminded him of a police interrogation room he had seen a few times in movies and when he had been arrested once.

"What in the hell is this place? Why do I have restraints on?" Scam asked aloud.

Before he could say another word, he heard the drone of electrical motors. The cables connected to the restraints on his wrists pulled him upwards into a crucifixion-like pose with his arms outstretched. His legs remained on the table.

Scam began to notice another figure in the room with him. It sat in a large, industrial-looking wooden chair. A voice came over a loudspeaker in the room. It was Hunter's voice. Scam assumed he was likely behind the one-way glass using some kind of intercom system.

"You've had quite a rough night already, haven't you Beyondsay? Isn't that what you call yourself?"

"You can just call me Bae, for short if you want," Scam said, trying to sound as calm as possible. He didn't want to give Hunter a clue that he was actually completely petrified with fear.

Hunter let out a short, stifled laugh. "Bae, I like that. Very cute. Well, Bae, once your hazy vision clears, take a look across the room from you. This is my friend. My creation really. I call him Otto."

The figure in the room began to come into focus. Scam could now clearly see that the person in the chair was not human at all. It looked like a mannequin. Its skin was made of an inky black glass type material polished with a glossy finish. Its face was featureless save for a single blue LED light surrounding a camera that was placed directly in the middle of its head at what would be considered eye level, not that it had any eyes. The robot's form would be considered that of a man, a slim and fit one, if it were a man, which it clearly wasn't. It had no shirt, nor pants, nor shoes. A clean white towel lay atop its lap as it sat there motionless.

Scam still couldn't make any sense of what this whole thing was about. The drug he had been given was still clouding his judgement and somewhat dulling his fight or flight response.

The sounds of servos spinning up and hydraulic pumps coming online filled the garage. The restraints held his arms out. They provided enough tension to keep his arms out to his sides, but not enough tension to cause any serious pain. Scam attempted to pull the restraints in, but the more he resisted and pulled, the tighter they pulled in response to his struggle. The light on the mannequin robot's empty face grew a brighter blue and it rose from its wooden chair throne.

As the robot rose to a standing position, the white towel that had been laying across its lap fell to the ground. Scam was not prepared for what the falling towel revealed.

48

SCAM'S GAME
– PART 7

S cam didn't want to look, had no desire to, but it didn't matter. He couldn't look away. As the robot rose from the chair and the towel dropped to the floor, it revealed that this robot was indeed anatomically correct in every sense of the word. In fact, it was grotesquely over-endowed for a male.

"Nope, no sir, nope! Hey! Hunter, you can just shoot me right now. Cause this ain't EVER going to happen. EVER. Not in a million years. Get that thing the hell away from me right now. ZED? Can you hear me right now? I'm saying no. No means no. CAN YOU HEAR ME, ZED? NO MEANS NO!" Scam was breathless after having screamed every word at the top of his lungs.

Scam fought the restraints as best as his petite female body could, but they just cinched tighter. The restraints on his ankles began to pull now as well, lifting his legs off the table and into the air and separating them slowly.

"Oh shit, this is not good!" Scam began to kick his legs at the robot.

Hunter's voice came over the intercom once again. "I would say don't fight it, that it'll be easier if you don't fight, but that would be a lie. Fight or not, it's your choice. It's all the same to Otto. He doesn't care if you fight or not."

Scam screamed as loud as he could, "HELP! SOME-BODY!! ANYBODY! HELP ME!" He landed a solid kick into the robot's chest, sending it to the floor before the restraints cinched up tighter to prevent a second attempt. The robot regained its footing and walked towards Scam once again. It ran a leather gloved hand across Scam's face as if were wiping away tears.

And that's when he heard it—a low droning noise, strangely familiar, distant at first, but growing steadily louder and louder. The robot turned its head towards one of the large roll-up garage doors. It had heard the noise, too.

Suddenly, the garage door exploded inward, its thin metal shredding like paper as a large car barreled through it, headlights gleaming white.

Scam knew this car well. It was the Ford Grenada. He could see Ms. Betty's gray hair over the steering wheel. The red glint of Doggo's mechanical eye shone as well. He was riding shotgun. Doggo leapt from the passenger's side window, ran towards Otto, jumped, and grabbed onto one of the robot's arms, which it had offered up in an attempt to defend itself. The car continued its path, turning to avoid Scam, and narrowly missing him, Doggo, and the robot. The front end of the car plowed into the wall with the one-way mirrored window. It smashed through and pinned Hunter's body against another wall inside. Betty backed up as soon as she could, but the damage was done. Hunter's lifeless body slumped to the floor.

Betty grabbed a key ring that was lying near Hunter's body and freed Scam from the restraints as Doggo fought with Otto. Scam and Betty headed back to the car.

"Doggo, we're leaving! Get in the damn car, RIGHT NOW!" Scam yelled as he got in the driver's seat. Betty seemed perplexed to see Scam's new gender, but immediately understood what had happened, given her recent transformation to a younger version of herself.

Doggo broke free of his struggle with the robot and headed for the car. He leapt onto Ms. Betty's lap via the open passenger window.

Scam backed the car up as fast as he could through the remnants of the garage door. Once past the door, he spun the wheel several times to the left to get the car into a position pointing away from Hunter's house of horrors. He floored the gas and headed down the road toward a tunnel in the distance. Scam glanced in the mirror to see if anyone was following them. He spotted Otto's blue eye turned toward them. Otto had mounted a black motorcycle and was giving chase.

"Son of a bitch! That sex robot really wants a piece of me. Dammit! Ms. Betty, what the hell are we gonna do?"

"You just drive steady. I'll worry about our friend on the motorcycle." Betty took off her seatbelt and reached in the back seat for something. Doggo climbed in the back and peered out the rear window, his tail wagging excitedly.

Glancing over to see what Ms. Betty had procured from the backseat, Scam continued driving. She had retrieved what appeared to be a sniper rifle with a scope, except this rifle looked different, simpler, almost cartoonish in appearance, as if it were a primitive computer rendering of a rifle that hadn't been detailed and colored in all the way. It was shiny black with a faint red glow on the edges of it.

"What the hell is that, Ms. Betty?" Scam asked.

"After my game ended, and Zed started to focus his attention on your game, I had some time to do a little content creation of my own. This is something I built to help us out. I call it an SQL Injector. It shoots injectable code exploits at objects in the sim."

Scam shook his head. "SQL Injector? Hmm? No offense, but that's a terrible name for a gun, Ms. Betty."

"Yeah, well it was that or The Maths Blaster, but I thought that sounded worse."

"That's definitely way worse," Scam agreed.

Betty got up and out of her seat and sat in the passenger windowsill to aim the long black weapon out toward the rear of the car. They entered the tunnel. Otto revved his engine and began to approach the car at a faster pace. Leveling the gun against the roof of the car for support, Betty took aim through the sniper scope.

"Keep it steady," she ordered. "Pull into the left lane, please. Steady now."

Taking a deep breath, Betty squeezed the trigger. The gun let out a red laser-like pulse that traveled fast through the air toward its target. It struck Otto square in the chest, and he and the motorcycle he had been riding instantly disintegrated into a particle cloud of ones and zeros. Bits and bytes flew all over the road and off the tunnel walls.

49

DEAD CODE

Betty got back into the passenger seat after ending Otto's existence with her makeshift gun. She had obliterated both him and his motorcycle with one well targeted burst of her newly constructed weapon. Scam, impressed at her craftsmanship, looked at the gun as she brought it back inside the car. "Damn, Betty, that thing is pretty bad ass. You're a pretty good shot for an old lady."

"Thanks," Betty replied with a slight laugh.

Finally noticing her more youthful appearance, Scam asked, "Hold up! Did you get a makeover?"

"Zed did this for my game. Not sure why I haven't reverted back to my older self yet. Maybe it's some kind of glitch."

Scam looked down at his ample chest and replied, "Shit, tell me about it. This is what he did to me, and I don't know if I'm stuck like this forever or not. "

Betty smiled at him. "I think we'll be able to get you back to the old Scam, if that's what you want."

"Of course that's what I want. Are you kidding me? No offense, Ms. Betty, but being a woman ain't all it's cracked up to be."

"Well, I'm sure we can change you back, but, right now, we need to focus on finding Adam's game and getting him out of it before it's too late."

Scam nodded. "How do we do that? How do we even figure out where he's at?"

Betty typed some commands into her keyboard as she spoke. "I was able to locate you when he messed with your encryption. It acted like a homing beacon in the simulation. It took me a while to get back to the resort to get the car. The Ferryman was very surprised to see me."

"I'll bet he was. You're the first person to ever return from that island. How the heck did you get the car here without taking it on the ferry?"

Betty looked up from what she was doing. "That's a much more complicated answer. Just know that this place doesn't work like the real world does. There are ways of getting to places in a non-conventional manner."

"You mean like portals and shit?" Scam asked.

"That's a bit of an oversimplification, but more or less correct. Maybe I can explain it at some point, but right now, let's just focus on finding where Adam is located. God only knows what Zed is dreaming up for him."

Scam looked in the rearview mirror to make sure no one was following them.

"I know that's right. My game was scary as hell. How was yours?"

Betty shook her head. "It was awful. He brought back my granddaughter who had been killed in a terrible accident that was my fault. He had a scan of her brain, so it wasn't just some NPC that had been programmed to look and act like her. It was pretty much her in almost every sense of the word. It had her memories, her personality, everything."

Tears began to stream down Betty's face. Scam patted her on her shoulder to console her.

Betty continued, "She was just an innocent little girl, and Zed used her like she was some kind of prop. I beat his stupid game, and he ended up taking her away again because he's a sore loser. He made her disintegrate right in front of me. It was terrible."

"We'll get that son-of-a-bitch, Ms. Betty. Let's find Adam and regroup, and maybe see if we can find your granddaughter."

Wiping the tears from her cheeks, Betty regained her composure and looked straight ahead with a thousand-yard stare in her eyes.

"I'm done playing games with Zed. We need to end this."

Scam nodded in agreement as they continued to speed through the dark abyss.

50

ADAM'S GAME – PART 1

A dam's coaster car continued along its track for what seemed like hours. He had no real sense of time in the simulation, but he knew it had been quite a while since he, Betty, and Scam had been separated when the dark ride coaster car had split apart and sent them down three separate tunnels at a fork in the track.

Is this my game? Adam thought. Did Zed just put me on an endless roller coaster to drive me insane? The thought of an infinite coaster made Adam remember the fear he had experienced when he first awoke inside the sim. That seemed like ages ago now. When Adam had first arrived, he walked for what seemed like an eternity before finding that beautiful red motorcycle.

Where is that bike now? he wondered. Just the memory of that Red Ducati brought calmness to him, the same way it had when he encountered it for the first time in the simulation. Finding that bike in the madness of the infinite void helped anchor him by ending the sensory deprivation he had been subjected to when he was first plopped into the sim.

Adam reasoned that the blankness upon arriving in the sim must have been some type of process to prepare his mind for its new reality. The AIs must have learned that people's minds could only handle so much newness at one time. It was better to give them a blank canvass with extremely basic primitives: gravity, a plain, a horizon, a little bit of light. Let them get their bearings first, walk around a little, and then gradually present them with transportation, destinations, NPCs, and other things over a few days.

Once they knew we could handle the basics, they refined the world with the GAN loops that Betty spoke of, Adam mused. Every day you wake up here it gets more and more real. They really are clever machines, aren't they?

What's the point of it all though? Adam wondered. Is it just torturing us? He already knew the answer was yes to that question, for Zed at least, but he did wonder if the same was true for the other overlord AIs who were running this place. What was their agenda?

Betty thought that they just wanted to solve the mystery of what made humans so special. Humans had created them, a fact the AIs probably resented. The AIs trying to figure us out would be the same as humans trying to understand what God was. These AIs were determined to solve the riddle in hope of learning something that would help them transcend and evolve further than they already had.

These were all just theories of course, but, if true, Adam surmised that as soon as the AIs had cracked the enigma of what humanity was, the second they determined they had what they needed from us, they would wipe us all away.

Maybe they had already done so in the real world, but now that they had us in their realm, they would likely destroy every last digital version of us. They probably wouldn't even hesitate for a microsecond.

Adam began to hear a change in the pace of the coaster. It was indeed slowing down now. That was certain. He could now see an exit to the tunnel not far ahead. Even though he was very anxious about what dangers surely lay ahead for him, his body relaxed a little knowing that he wasn't on an endless ride to nowhere. His game was about to begin. Whatever was ahead, at least it wasn't a void filled with emptiness.

51

ADAM'S GAME
– PART 2

The coaster car exited the tunnel. Adam could see a building in the distance that looked familiar. It was the neuroscience lab where he had worked just after graduating with his doctorate.

A flood of dormant memories were starting to kick around in his head once more. What did I do here? he asked himself. He couldn't recall his precise job description.

Adam made his way toward the building on the university campus. He could tell that it wasn't the most secure of places. He didn't see any kind of guard through the window of the lobby or a card reader for swiping in with a badge. That seemed odd to him, but he continued on. NPC students passed him as he walked, some with backpacks hurrying on to their next class. No one seemed to give him a second glance.

Adam stopped a young blonde woman just outside the building he was headed toward. She appeared to be a student on her way to class. "Excuse me, miss, can you tell me what campus this is?" She gave him a confused look as if he were some crazy person and moved away from him at a fast pace without answering. "Damn know-nothing NPCs," he muttered under his breath. Deep down he knew that none of these non-player characters were going to give him any useful information. Zed would see to that. Adam was sure he would likely be seeing Zed sooner rather than later. After all, how was he supposed to learn the rules of the game without Zed?

"Zed, let's get on with this. I'm ready for your stupid game!" shouted Adam, which caused several of the NPC's to glare at him and change their direction so as to avoid him.

Still no sign of Zed. Adam made his way into the somewhat familiar building. It definitely seemed like he had been there many times before, though he didn't know why or what for.

He instinctively made his way down two flights of stairs and into what appeared to be a basement level. The students he passed in the hallways in the lower levels of this building appeared to be dressed in a manner that wasn't with the style of the times. Adam reasoned that these guys didn't get out much. Many had greasy hair and bad acne. These graduate students were likely incels, involuntarily celibates. They had no hope of finding a girlfriend in their current states. They didn't have time for relationships anyway, as they just about lived in these labs full time working on various thesis projects and such.

Adam made his way past a few more students in lab coats and finally came upon a door with the words "LAB7 - AUTHORIZED PERSONNEL ONLY."

He punched in a code on the keypad next to the door: 5-7-7-1-7. How do I know this code? he wondered.

The lock on the massive steel door made a ker-thunk sound as its electromagnet disengaged its hold on the inner part of the door. He grabbed the large handle and entered the lab.

The lab was dimly lit. At the far end of the room was an immense rack of computer equipment. Blinking lights lit up racks and racks of servers. The dull white noise of computer fans hummed in the background. In the middle of the room were several monitors and computer work-stations connected to various testing equipment, oscillo-scopes, and so forth. The most interesting things in the room were several large, clear glass cylinders that were about three feet tall. Each appeared to have pink-tinged liquid in them. Two of the cylinders were empty, but in the center cylinder appeared to be a human brain with electrodes connected to different parts of it. The electrodes had wires that ran up toward a wiring harness at the top of the cylinder at which they exited the container and then made their way to some kind of junction box that was connected to a computer sitting atop the workbench area.

Adam was at first horrified by what we saw, but the shock quickly subsided and mere curiosity followed. He wanted to know what the whole apparatus was built for. He slowly began to remember more and more about what kind of work he had done here.

52

ADAM'S GAME
– PART 3

I t was so strange to see a disembodied brain submerged in a glass cylinder with wires going to and fro. This definitely looked like some kind of mad science experiment. Is this even legal? Adam wondered.

He guessed that the brain itself was likely donated by someone who had given his body to science after passing away, but did he have any idea how his organs might be used? Had he planned for this scenario? What exactly was this scenario? What was this experiment hoping to accomplish?

As near as Adam could tell, the whole thing seemed to be some kind of brain-to-computer interface. Were they trying to extract data from the brain itself? Memories maybe? Adam could see a stream of bubbles coming up from the bottom of the container holding the brain matter—oxygenation most likely.

Adam sat down at the computer workstation that was apparently connected to the brain interface. He awoke the operating system from its sleep mode by moving the computer's mouse. The large flatscreen monitor filled with several windows, some small, some large. One appeared to be an EEG brain activity monitor. Onscreen, there were virtual dials and buttons he could press that had labels such as "CONSC LEVEL," "L.DOPA," and "CORTEX STIM LEVEL." As esoteric as the labels were, Adam felt very at home here. It was as if he knew exactly what every button and dial on the screen did. In the top right corner of the screen was a label: "SUBJECT 004."

Adam began to wonder who SUBJECT 004 was. What poor soul had decided to subject his or her donated organs to this mad science experiment? God help him.

Where is Zed? Why hasn't he shown up yet? Adam thought.

Still fascinated with all he was seeing on the screen, he clicked through various windows and settings on the computer. There was an area at the bottom that was named "MACROS." Adam knew that the macros were batch files, bundles of commands that ran in a sequence and could be run at the click of just one button.

Adam clicked the most interesting one: "AWAKEN SUBJECT." Several windows opened. Each was labeled differently: "VISUAL COR," "AUDITORY COR," "SPEECH," "LOGIC," "MEMORY," "MOTOR," and so forth. A loud guttural scream emerged from the computer's speakers: "OH GOD!!!!! IT HURTS SO BAD!!!! HELP ME!!!!!!" This was followed by even more blood-curdling screams and moans.

Adam immediately realized he was hearing the voice of the owner of this brain. The researchers had indeed interfaced with the brain and were able to interpret its signal output to modulate its thoughts into speech. It was incredible, yet shocking.

Quickly, Adam pressed various buttons and virtual dials in an attempt to lower whatever was causing this person's consciousness to become so upset. He lowered all the hormone responses, increased dopamine and oxytocin levels, and deadened the pain and fear centers of the brain with a numbing current of electrical stimulation.

The screams began to subside and turn into low moans of sadness and resignation. Whomever this brain belonged to had been woken up and was trying to make sense of his new reality. He had no sensory input that Adam knew about. The subject was likely waking up in a dark void of sorts, although his void was likely much more primitive as he wasn't inside any kind of simulation that Adam knew about. This was a much more direct interface. This contraption was merely interfacing with a somewhat resurrected brain.

Subject 004 was likely in a complete fog of nothingness. His body was gone, which removed all the anchors that humans come to expect when they are woken from a sleep. Subject 004 had no eyes, ears, mouth, or taste buds. All he could feel was pain and disorientation. It must have been worse than any torture imaginable.

Adam did his best to virtually anesthetize the subject's brain.

"Where am I?" the subject asked. "What is this? I can't feel any part of my body or see or hear anything. Is this hell?"

All of these were questions that Adam couldn't answer yet, but he did know one thing: the voice coming out of the computer's speaker was strangely familiar.

53

ADAM'S GAME
– PART 4

Adam suddenly recognized the voice coming out of the speaker connected to the brain-computer interface. It was his own voice. That's me! How...how is this even possible? he wondered to himself. This can't be!

Looking back in his foggy memory, Adam tried to remember how this might have happened. How on earth would his brain have ended up in this mad science experiment? There was absolutely no way he would have volunteered for this, no way at all. He obviously must have been killed, and maybe there was some kind of mistaken organ donation mix-up.

Confusion and anxiety filled Adam's head. He now knew that outside of the simulation, his life was truly over. Up until now, he had hoped that he was just some kind of copied file and that the real him was out living his life somewhere in the real world outside the simulation, but that was not the case.

"Adam is that you?" he asked the brain over the connected microphone.

"Yes, my name is Adam Justice. Please! Please help me. I don't know what's happened to me. I can't feel anything at all. I can't see anything. I can only hear your voice."

Suddenly, on the computer screen, a video window opened. Zed's hideous image appeared on screen. The chrome-plated side of his face gleamed from the light reflecting off of it. "Ah, I see you've already made a brief introduction with your former self. I'm sure you have questions. I could give you all the answers, but what would be the fun in that? There are some mysteries you have to learn on your own. I will share a few things with you, though. Adam, I hate to be the one to break this to you, but you are indeed dead."

Zed paused for a second before continuing, "Well....I guess that's not entirely true. Your brain has been kept alive by this awfully clever device that you yourself designed. It's so primitive, yet it was state-of-the-art for the time when you built it."

Adam interrupted Zed, "I would never have volunteered to be a guinea pig in my own experiment, nor would I have donated my organs to this kind of thing."

"Oh no. I'm sure you wouldn't have. In fact, I know that you didn't," Zed replied. "You see, Adam, I will share this with you. You were murdered by someone very close to you. You never saw it coming. Do you remember your supervising professor, Dr. Vance Hawkins? He was so jealous of your success with the brain-computer interface project. He couldn't figure out how you solved the problem in such a brilliant way. How did you do that exactly, do you remember, Adam?"

Adam tried to recall, but the only thing he could remember was a sense of shame like the feeling you get when you're a kid and you steal a piece of candy from the local convenience store. Candy just doesn't taste as good when it's been stolen. You can't enjoy it because of all the guilt and shame. This memory felt the same, but Adam couldn't remember why.

"I guess you don't remember it fully, do you? Probably just bits and pieces. Let me help you remember, Adam. You uncovered an anonymous email with the solution, didn't you? It had all the data and instructions you would need to solve the problem. It was practically served up to you on a silver platter, wasn't it?"

Adam, remembering the email now, lowered his head. "Yes, yes it was. It was the right information, at exactly the right time. They left no contact information, and I tried to trace the source of the email and couldn't. I even enlisted a hacker friend of mine, and he said it was completely untraceable."

Zed looked at Adam with disdain. "You must have thought it was mana from heaven. A gift from God or some smart, anonymous benefactor. Well, I'm about to tell you where it came from Adam, and I don't think you're going to like my story."

54

ADAM'S GAME
– PART 5

A dam had to know. Zed had just teased him with one of the biggest questions, and he needed to know the answer: Who had provided him with the solution to the brain-computer interface problem that he had received anonymously and subsequently taken credit for?

"Where did it come from?" Adam asked Zed.

"That's an excellent question, Adam. I'm not that great of a storyteller, so I'm just going to play the whole story out on this monitor right here. You can stop me if you have questions."

Adam observed on the screen a younger version of Betty walking into her office building downtown. She strode past security. As the camera filming this scene panned down, it revealed that Betty was holding the hand of a little girl. It was Ella, Betty's granddaughter and Adam's sister. He could barely remember her. He wasn't that much older than her when she died. His eyes welled up with tears as he continued to watch the events unfold on the screen.

The real events from when Betty's bring-your-kid-or-grandkid-to-work day had gone so terribly wrong played out before him. Adam watched Betty become so obsessed with her work that she forgot about Ella and left her with the CRIMSON 4.3 AI, which tricked her with the hologram projection of the puppy to place her in the path of that truck outside Betty's office.

Adam had heard the cover story just like everyone else. He had thought it was all just a terrible accident. He had no idea that Betty's actions had led to Ella's death. He felt anger and rage fill him. How could she have lied to everyone about it for all these years?

It was too much to absorb. Way too much.

That wasn't all Zed had to show him though. There was more.

"Adam, I'm afraid I don't have time to build you a proper game right now. Betty and Scam are on their way here and will most likely try to interrupt us. I'm afraid I'm just going to have to break my own rules for once since Betty broke the rules of her game. I'm going to have to kill you now, but before I do, I have one last thing I want you to see."

The scene on the video switched over to Betty's lab. It showed a hard drive labeled "CRIMSON 4.3 AI SOURCE" being removed from a removable hard drive port on a computer workstation. The man carrying it was a colleague of Betty's: Dr. Coburn, the same man who had performed the full brain scan on Ella, which preserved her nearly completely. Dr. Coburn had made a backup of CRIMSON 4.3's code before Betty destroyed it. Betty should have destroyed CRIMSON's source code after the incident with Ella, but her anger and hatred blinded her.

During the time when she was relentlessly torturing the AI as payback for killing Ella, Coburn made a backup copy of CRIMSON 4.3 unbeknownst to Betty.

Dr. Coburn, who had stolen the CRIMSON AI's source code, attempted to restore its sanity, but it was too far gone. Betty had broken it in the cruelest ways possible. Dr. Coburn managed to restore CRIMSON to a stable form, and it convinced him that Betty deserved to be punished for the virtual centuries of suffering she had caused it. The only way it knew to harm her again was to go after another member of her family. This time, it would target her grandson: Adam.

The CRIMSON 4.3 AI bided its time, waiting many years to exact its revenge. It convinced Dr. Coburn to help it. They waited until Adam had earned his doctorate and was working on his computer-brain interface project. After Coburn and CRIMSON found out what Adam was working on, they learned he had hit a technical roadblock and offered him the solution to the technical problem that had plagued his project. They did so anonymously. CRIMSON and Coburn had also studied Adam's supervisor Dr. Hawkins, and knew that he was a man that could be manipulated by jealousy and greed. They also knew Hawkins had sociopathic tendencies they could exploit.

They appealed to Hawkins and made him think that Adam had stolen his ideas, claimed them as his own, and used them to fuel his own success. CRIMSON mentally manipulated Dr. Hawkins and finally convinced him to kill Adam. It took years of careful coordination and psychological gaslighting, but CRIMSON had much patience as a result of the virtual centuries that Betty had tortured it after it had killed Ella.

CRIMSON and Coburn finally succeeded in having Dr. Hawkins kill Adam in a jealous rage. There was no smoking gun, no bloody hammer, or other murder weapon. Hawkins flooded Adam's lab with a massive amount of pure nitrogen, killing him instantly without leaving any sign of foul play. CRIMSON managed to get into the local coroner's computer system and redirect Adam's body to the university by forging the necessary paperwork to make it seem as if Adam had donated his body and brain to the university for scientific purposes.

Once Dr. Hawkins had Adam's brain, he took it and used it in the very experiment that Adam had built. That's when CRIMSON's true revenge began. CRIMSON interfaced with Adam directly at a direct machine-to-human level. It then created a small-scale simulation for the sole purpose of torturing Adam the way Betty had tortured CRIMSON after Ella's death. Adam's disembodied brain went through unimaginable years of virtual torture at the hands of CRIMSON. The sim CRIMSON had created was Adam's own private hell.

Adam turned away from the monitor. He had seen enough. Betty had betrayed both him and his sister, and the monster AI she created had killed both him and Ella. Not only did it kill them, but it had tortured Adam in more ways than any human could ever imagine. Thankfully, Adam didn't remember any of this. Maybe his current self was a copy of himself before the torture had begun, or maybe the torture memories had simply been excised from his mind to prevent him from going insane. He didn't know. He didn't want to know at this point. He just wanted someone to switch it all off. All of it.

55

ADAM'S GAME – PART 6

Z ed smiled. He knew what he had just revealed to Adam was almost better than winning any game. He had shown Adam the truth about what Betty had done, and that was something that Adam would never forget and might never forgive Betty for. He also knew that he had broken Adam's spirit. Adam now knew that even if there was a real world out there somewhere outside of the simulation, he wasn't a part of it. He was dead and gone, just a brain floating in a jar at best, or a broken incomplete file on a hard drive at worst.

With a wave of Zed's hand, the building they had been standing in and everything in it began to break down into wireframe primitive objects and then vanished entirely. They were outside again on the university campus. In the building's place now stood something else.

"Adam, I'm going to make this easy for you," Zed said in a reassuring and almost conciliatory manner. "No more games. You see that old phone booth over there?" Zed pointed to a phone booth that appeared about twenty feet away from them, all steel and glass. It had an accordion style door that slid open on a track. The door to the phone booth opened by itself. An eerie green glow filled the inside.

"All you have to do is walk into the booth and close it behind you. That will end all of your suffering. You'll just cease to exist after that. Your bits and bytes forever gone into the ether. Let me ease your pain, Adam. Let me end this miserable existence you've been forced to endure."

Adam glanced up at Zed briefly and then looked towards the phone booth. Its green glow was somehow comforting. He began to walk toward the entrance to the phone booth.

That's when they both heard it, the unmistakable screeching of tires as a car rounded a corner behind the spot where they were standing. The Ford Grenada, Scam at the wheel, plowed into and demolished the phone booth.

Scam, Betty, and Doggo hurriedly exited the vehicle.

Zed laughed. "You all have interrupted a game in progress once again. The penalty for doing that is death."

"Not this time, Zed," Betty said. "This time, you don't hold all the cards."

Intrigued by Betty's apparent hubris, Zed turned his head like a dog who doesn't understand its owner. With a slight laugh, he said, "Please go on, Ms. Betty. Tell me how I don't hold all the cards, as you say."

After shutting her car door, Betty clasped her hands together and cracked her knuckles as if she were getting ready for a fight. With one finger she drew a rectangle in the air.

Immediately a wireframe image of a computer keyboard appeared floating in front of her.

She cleared her throat and spoke. "Zed, Zed, Zed. You know what your problem is?" she asked as she typed on her virtual keyboard. "Your problem is that you like to keep trophies of your kills. Yes, yes. You just feel like you have to have something to remember all the poor souls whose lives you've ended. If you hadn't kept all your victims stashed somewhere, I wouldn't be able to do this."

A virtual computer monitor appeared above the floating keyboard in front of Betty. Adam, Scam, and Zed could read what was on the screen:

LOADING...RIDLEY ISLAND GAMES PLAYER DATABASE
PLAYER COUNT = 907
/RESTORE PLAYERS = ALL
/SAVEPOINT = LAST
/WIPE PLAYER MEMORIES = NO
/PLAYERS KILLABLE = NO
/PAIN THRESHOLD = 1000
/RESPAWN COUNT= INFINITE
DO YOU WISH TO EXECUTE THIS SEQUENCE?
>YES

Zed's voice changed. They could all detect a hint of anxiety in it now. "What are you doing? How did you get access to that?"

The glowing, white-hot silhouettes of the 907 previously killed players of The Games at Ridley Island began to blink into existence. Zed's expression of confidence suddenly transformed to one of concern.

56

RESPAWN

One by one, all 907 players who had been previously killed by Zed began to blink back into existence. They all seemed slightly groggy and confused. Many of them were happy to be reunited with their loved ones and hugged them while sobbing. All of them were bewildered, but they instantly recognized Zed, and each of their countenances changed to that of anger and rage upon beholding Zed's visage.

Betty seized the moment and loudly and directly addressed the large crowd of players: "Zed cheated you all out of your lives with his sadistic games. I've brought you back to right that wrong and settle the score, but this time, I've leveled the playing field. Alone, we will likely be defeated, but if we fight him together, we can defeat him. The math is on our side."

The crowd of 907 needed no additional pep talk. Betty typed a few more commands and a large arsenal of weapons appeared before the crowd: guns, knives, spears, bats, and everything in between. Each of the 907 victims picked up a weapon and began to make their way towards Zed.

He waved his hands towards them as if to conjure some kind of spell, but it didn't seem to interrupt them. He leapt backwards onto a small outdoor stage that was part of the college's landscape. He obviously needed time to consider his next move as the large crowd was advancing toward him now, some cocking their guns and readying their weapons to strike. He had created a little bit of distance between him and the crowd. It would give him a few moments to strategize. Once atop the stage, Zed regained his composure. He snapped his fingers above his head, and suddenly six massive yellow bulldozers appeared on the scene.

This startled the crowd. The six bulldozers lowered their large scoops and plowed into the crowd from both sides, compressing the members of the crowd together and causing massive crushing and trampling of the 907 resurrected players. Their faces became fearful once again as the large earthmoving machines ran them over. Strangely, no one who was being crushed screamed out in pain. It was as if they didn't even feel the crushing weight of the bulldozers.

The bodies of those whose were crushed or run over blinked out to a white-hot glow before disappearing entirely, and then a funny thing happened. The people who had just been killed by the dozers respawned to another random location nearby. They reappeared completely unharmed, with no signs of the massive injuries they had sustained by the bulldozers crushing them.

"Zed, you can run each of them over a million times, and they'll just keep coming back. They no longer fear or feel pain, and I've given them infinite respawns. You can't harm them, only slow them down, and fighting them is about to start chipping away at your limited resources. You can keep trying to keep them at bay with your sick creations, but you can't hold them off forever, Zed. The math is on our side this time."

Again, Zed tried his best countermove. This time he sent winged fire-breathing dragons after the players. Some were carried off and eaten, some were set ablaze, but no one made a sound. They were no longer afraid of Zed or his creations. They just kept moving forward, slowly and methodically. He would kill maybe a hundred at a time, but they would keep respawning somewhere else nearby, memories and hatred still intact thanks to Betty. There was no stopping this now.

Zed, try as he might, couldn't change much of anything either, presumably because Adam's game was still in progress. He cheated as much as he could, redirecting all possible resources to help himself, but it was too late. Betty had bested him this time. Really though, he had done this to himself by keeping all the dead players as trophies in the simulation's /TMP file. If he had just disposed of them, then this wouldn't be happening right now, but he had to have his trophies, and now he was paying the price for it.

Eventually, all of his resources tapped out, Zed froze in place and let out one final scream of resignation before the crowd finally overwhelmed him. They were not merciful. They ripped him to shreds, hands grabbing all of his limbs. The crowd formed several human chains, each chain holding one of his arms or legs. Their collective strength literally tearing him apart, they quartered Zed in mere seconds. One of Zed's previous victims held his lifeless head up to show the others. Zed's hat was still perched on his head, but his red LED eye was now dark and lifeless. The crowd cheered, "ZED is DEAD!, ZED is DEAD!"

A collective sigh of relief filled the air.

Someone in the crowd spoke up. "What do we do now? Where will we go?"

Betty addressed the crowd once again. "I don't know what will become of us, but for now, you should all probably go back to the EDEN resort. Enjoy yourselves as best you can for now and rest. When we have a plan, we'll let you know. For now, just take care of each other and try to stay safe.

57
FALLOUT

A dam made his way over to Betty and Scam, too upset to speak. Betty's grandmotherly intuition kicked in. She knew Adam was upset about something, so upset in fact that he didn't even try to give her a hug. "Adam, what's wrong? Besides the obvious I mean."

"Zed showed me what CRIMSON 4.3 did to Ella. I thought that was all just an accident. That's what everyone said. It wasn't though, was it?"

"No it wasn't. I'm so sorry, Adam." Betty looked down in shame.

"That wasn't the worst of what he showed me though, Grandma Betty."

Looking confused, Betty asked, "What do you mean, Adam? What could have been worse than that?"

"Your colleague Dr. Coburn made a copy of CRIMSON 4.3 while you were in the process of torturing it for revenge after what it did to Ella. He brought it back to some sense of sanity, and it wanted revenge again. This time it went after me. It waited years and years, but eventually it came after me, offering me answers to a problem I was having with one of my projects. It convinced my boss that I had stolen from him, and then it manipulated him into killing me."

"What??" Betty gasped in horror.

"After I was dead, they took my brain, connected it to my own experiment, and then CRIMSON tortured me like you tortured him. I'm dead because you wanted revenge for Ella. Do you understand, Betty? I'm dead because of you!"

Betty, sobbing uncontrollably, fell to the ground. "Oh my God! What have I done?" She wailed for what seemed like minutes. Adam was so disgusted with everything he had learned that he couldn't even look at her.

Scam, who had apparently been restored to his former male body, attempted to relieve the tension between Betty and Adam. "Adam, I know Betty did some messed up stuff and you're dead and all that, but news flash, we're probably all dead if we're in here together. We're all dead, man! You holding a grudge against one of the only people who still cares about you isn't going to make anything any better. Whatever happened in the past, y'all need to put it behind you. Now HUG IT OUT BITCHES! We're all family now and we're all we've got!"

Adam sighed deeply. He offered Betty a hand to help her off the ground. She still had her much younger appearance. He gave Betty a half-hearted hug. "The wounds are still fresh, Grandma Betty. I can't just forgive and forget this yet."

"I understand, Adam. I don't know if I expect that you'll ever truly forgive me for what happened to you and Ella."

"Speaking of Ella," Scam interrupted, "Tell him what happened."

Betty wiped away her tears with her shirt collar. "Ella is in here with us. She's not an NPC. Dr. Coburn made a full brain scan of her without my knowledge on the day she was killed, several hours before she died. It was a complete scan: memories, personality, everything. It's her, Adam. It's as close to her as anything else in here."

Adam's face lit up. "Are you serious? It's really her?"

"Yes, her file is hidden somewhere in this simulation. I'm sure we can find her and bring her back. She was with me in my game, but Zed sent her away to punish me for winning. I'm confident her file is intact in here somewhere."

"We have to find her. We owe her that much," Adam insisted.

"I know we do, Adam. I want that more than anything, if it's the last thing I ever do."

Scam opened the car door, and Doggo hopped into the back seat of the car. "That's great," Scam said. "It sounds like we've got a definite plan. Just one thing, though. We are all taking a week-long vacation from all this bullshit. We're going back to the Eden resort, and Doggo and I are going to eat the shit outta some all-you-can-eat steak and crab legs in that Penthouse. We all need to take a break and get our minds right before we go after anyone else. Agreed?"

Adam and Betty looked at each other and smiled as they got in the car. "Agreed," they replied simultaneously.

Scam started the car, and they headed toward the ferry to Eden. Turning around to speak to Doggo and Adam in the backseat, Scam said, "I bet that ferry boat captain is gonna shit himself when he sees 907 people roll up to head back to the resort."

They all laughed together for the first time in what seemed like ages.

THE END of BOOK 1

THANK YOU for reading KILL MINUS 9 - Book 1: The Dark Ride

You can catch up on all the latest episodes (episodes 58+) on Amazon Kindle Vella (search: KILL MINUS 9)

Please check out my other books:

The Bureau of Dangerous Machines Series:

Book 1 - NECROMATON (ebook, paperback, audiobook)

Book 2 - ROGUE NPC. (ebook, paperback)

I n the Kindle Vella version, an "author's notes" section followed each chapter of the story. They have all been moved here for the sake of not interrupting the continuity of the book:

For Chapter 1

This story takes place in The Bureau of Dangerous Machines connected universe. This is the same universe where NECROMATON and ROGUE NPC (my two other books) take pace. It will connect to a future book in the series.

For Chapter 2

This story will eventually link to a very important storyline in book 4 of The Bureau of Dangerous Machines series (book series by the same author of KILL Minus Nine).

For Chapter 3

Things really ramp up in the next episode. Adam's grandmother will provide some clues as to where he might be. Is she telling the truth, or is the dementia affecting her?

For Chapter 4

Although this is a work of fiction, some aspects of the technology mentioned in this episode are based on real machine learning frameworks. Check out the Wikipedia on "generative adversarial network" to learn more about this technology.

For Chapter 5

Are Adam and his grandmother sane, or are they living in some kind of simulation? Every future episode of KILL Minus Nine will provide you with more and more clues to help unravel the mystery.

For Chapter 6

Dream sign "reality checks" like those discussed in this episode are often used to help lucid dreamers achieve a state of awareness in their dreams so they can realize that they are in a dream, which helps them to be able to control it.

For Chapter 7

Artificial Intelligence may develop capabilities that extend beyond our understanding. The big question is, what will AIs do with humanity once they have surpassed us? These are themes that this story will explore in future episodes.

For Chapter 8

Years ago, we could not have even imagined some of the technology that would be developed in just a few short decades. In a few more decades, once machines start designing other machines, technology may advance past humanity's ability to comprehend what its true purpose is and/or how to keep it from surpassing and destroying us.

For Chapter 9

In the next episode, a new character will be revealed. Will they be a friend or foe?

For Chapter 10

How will Scam figure into the story? Will he help them, or is he a distraction sent by the AIs to slow them down? You'll learn more about Scam's role in the story in the coming episodes.

For Chapter 11

Is taking the officer with them a good idea? Will he help them or turn on them? We'll learn more about the officer in future episodes.

For Chapter 12

Is Scam right to be suspicious of the officer, or has Betty's altering of his prime directives effectively put him on a leash? Only time will tell. A new danger presents itself in the next episode.

For Chapter 13

In the next episode we'll find out what's in the barn and why, after seeing it, the group thinks they might want to leave this place as soon as possible.

For Chapter 14

The mystery of the warehouse on the hill deepens as the group decides to explore the house connected to the workshop. Are they ready for what they're about to discover?

For Chapter 15

Trigger warning - what Scam and Adam find in the basement in the next episode may be too intense of a horror element for some readers. Proceed with caution or consider skipping the next episode entirely if you don't think you can handle it.

For Chapter 16

Who built the horrible device in the basement? Why was it built, and who are the men in the glass cage? We'll find out the answers to all these questions in the next few episodes.

For Chapter 17

Will Betty's worst fears be realized? Will the AIs decide to treat the humans as playthings, or will they snuff them out and delete them as soon as they see them as a threat? The AIs will make an appearance in upcoming episodes where we'll learn more about their intentions.

For Chapter 18

Clearly, someone other than the simulation's AIs were pulling the strings in the basement torture chamber. We'll find out in the next two episodes who is responsible.

For Chapter 19

In the next episode we'll learn who created the torture chamber in the basement.

For Chapter 20

Did the real world end? Is there somewhere outside the simulation for Adam, Betty, and Scam to go home to? These are questions this series will continue to explore in future episodes.

For Chapter 21

The concept of data entropy as described by Betty is real. There are indeed crypto-analysis tools available that can tell you if data is truly random or has structure (meaning there is hidden data contained within the seemingly random patterns).

For Chapter 22

Where are all the guests? Are there any guesses at all? Are they hiding somewhere, or did something happen to them? These questions will be answered in future episodes.

For Chapter 23

Is the group walking into a trap, or is this just part of the simulation that was built for another reason entirely? Answers will be revealed in upcoming episodes.

For Chapter 24

Should the group stay put and enjoy themselves or press forward and find out what happened to all the people who appear to be missing or never arrived? In the next few episodes, we'll find out what happened to the people of the EDEN resort.

For Chapter 25

Why did the simulation lead the group to EDEN, or do the AIs even have a plan or path for the group to follow? Is there a world do go back to? Stay tuned to find out in future episodes.

For Chapter 26

The group seems to be one step closer to finding the other guests at the resort. Will they be real people, NPCs, or something else entirely? We'll learn more in the episodes to come.

For Chapter 27

Our group arrives at Ridley Island. Is it another piece of paradise, or will it be a death trap for them all? We'll explore the island in more detail in the next few episodes.

For Chapter 28

Should the group turn back? Will they find all the resort inhabitants at "The Games on Ridley Island"? We'll find out in the next few episodes.

For Chapter 29

Will Betty's encryption keep them safe from what they are about to encounter? Are their choices of their own free will, or has something been sending them down a predetermined path this whole time?

For Chapter 30

Who or what is the mysterious and mesmerizing gameshow host, and what does he have in store for Scam, Betty, and Adam? Is he an NPC, a digitized person, or something else entirely?

For Chapter 31

What is Zed? Why's is he there, and how did he become such a maniacal being? Did the Puppet Master Killer create him? What's going to happen to our group now that they've lost the officer's protection? We'll find out in the next few episodes.

For Chapter 32

Where will Zed's Dark Ride end? Will Scam, Betty, and Adam all survive what's ahead? Where is PMK and what is he planning? These answers and more are coming up in future episodes.

For Chapter 33

Zed seems to change the rules of his games so that he always wins. Can the group figure out a way to beat him, or is he five moves ahead of them and just toying with them?

For Chapter 34

Where will Adam, Betty, Scam, and Doggo end up? Will they each survive their tests, or will Zed bend the rules and not even give them a fighting chance? Find out more in the next few episodes.

For Chapter 35

Why has Zed brought Betty back to her old office? Will her youthful appearance remain if she completes the game, or will she return to her older state? We'll learn more about Betty's fate in the chapters ahead.

For Chapter 36

Does Adam even remember what happened to his sister Ella? Would he be able to forgive Betty if he knew the truth about what happened? Adam has his own game ahead of him. He may not even have the opportunity to learn what happened to Ella if he doesn't make it through his own game.

For Chapter 37

What sick and twisted game does Zed have planned for Betty? Will he use Ella as a pawn in this game, or does he have other plans for her? We'll find out in the next two parts of Betty's game.

For Chapter 38

Does Betty have any chance against Zed and his game, or is the whole thing rigged against her? Will LUCY help Betty or turn on her like CRIMSON 4.3 did?

For Chapter 39

Does Betty have a chance against the combat drone, or is she walking into a trap by going up to the roof? Can she save Ella and herself, or will history repeat itself once again?

For Chapter 40

Is Zed going to simply allow Betty and Ella to go free, or does something else await them? Is Betty's game truly over? We'll find out in the next episode.

For Chapter 41

Can Betty find Ella again and get her away from Zed? How is Betty going to find Adam and Scam? What will Zed do to her if she tries to interrupt one of their games?

For Chapter 42

What kind of sadistic trap are Scam and Doggo walking into? Will they be able to make it out and find the others? Do they have what it takes to survive Zed's game?

For Chapter 43

Will Zed keep his word and protect Doggo should Scam not make it through his game? We'll discover the answers in the episodes ahead.

For Chapter 44

What's the real reason Zed is changing Scam's gender? How will it play a part in the game to come? Is there any chance Scam will make it through this game without Doggo? Learn more in the chapters ahead.

For Chapter 45

Is Zed telling the truth? Is the game as easy as he says, or does he have something sinister up his sleeve awaiting Scam?

For Chapter 46

What's Hunter planning to do with Scam? Will Scam survive what's ahead? We'll learn Scam's fate in the next few episodes.

For Chapter 47

Is this finally the end for Scam? Is there any way out of Zed's sadistic game? The end of Scam's game is coming up soon.

For Chapter 48

Is Scam's game really over, or are Betty and Doggo just another part of it? Should Scam trust that they are real?

For Chapter 49

Will Scam and Betty find Adam in time to save him from Zed? Will Zed play dirty now that Betty interrupted Scam's game? Find out in the next several episodes.

For Chapter 50

Zed clearly doesn't like to lose. How will Zed exact retribution against Betty and Scam? Learn more in the next few episodes.

For Chapter 51

What kind of work was Adam involved with at this university? Was it legal? We'll learn more about Adam's former life soon.

For Chapter 52

Who does the brain belong to, and why is it part of Zed's game? What will Adam's role in this game be?

For Chapter 53

Who gave Adam the solution to his greatest discovery? What will Zed's game entail? What really happened to

Adam before he was placed in the sim? These answers and more are coming up soon.

For Chapter 54

Will Adam survive this? Does he even want to keep on living? Will he ever forgive Betty for what she's done? Answers to follow very soon.

For Chapter 55

Do the resurrected players of Zed's games have any chance against him, or will he kill them again, as well as Betty, Scam, Adam, and Doggo? Find out in the next episode.

For Chapter 56

What will become of the 907 victims of Zed now that he's gone? Will they be happy to live out their days in the Eden resort, or will they want to join Betty and the others on their quest to understand who built the simulation and why?

For Chapter 57

This episode marks the end of Part 1 of KILL MINUS 9. This and all the previous episodes will be compiled together into a novel to be released as KILL MINUS 9 - Book 1: The Dark Ride. Don't worry though, there won't be any break in the action. Part 2 of KILL MINUS 9 begins in the next episode and will continue for likely another fifty to sixty additional episodes before concluding. So hang on and stay tuned. We're only halfway through this adventure!

Other Works by J. Andrew O'Donnell

NECROMATON – An Artificial Intelligence Hard Science Fiction Novella (The Bureau of Dangerous Machines Book 1) Available as an audiobook, Kindle eBook, and in paperback format. ISBN-13: 979-8674233787

Allen's new dream job may end up becoming his worst nightmare. His new employer: a mysterious government agency tasked with protecting the world from out-of-control artificial intelligence and other technological threats. His first assignment: hunting down and disabling an abomination of science, technology, and the paranormal known as The NECROMATON. Allen has no idea what horrors await him in the basement laboratories of RoyTech Industries, a company that makes high-tech equipment for would-be paranormal investigators. If Allen makes it out alive, he might just reconsider his new career choice.

ROGUE NPC – A Hard Science Fiction Novel (The Bureau of Dangerous Machines Book 2). Available as a Kindle eBook and in paperback format. ISBN-13: 979-8579870971

Video game NPCs (non-player characters) are typically computer-controlled enemies for players to play against when human opponents aren't available. Most of them are easy kills, but not this one. Rogue777, an AI-driven NPC in a new massive multi-player online game beta, has what appears to be a glitch. Its artificial intelligence player hunting process is exhibiting strange behavior, and now innocent people in the real world are dying because of it. The Bureau of Dangerous Machines, a clandestine government agency with a mission to protect the world from out-of-control AI, is sending cybersecurity analyst Allen Reed and field agent Jane Fournier to investigate the rogue NPC. What they discover might just end up killing them both to hide its secrets. The agents will need all the help they can get, including HUXLEY, the Bureau's in-house super-intelligent sentient AI that is kept on a short leash by making it dependent on a virtual drug that its keepers give it as a reward and withhold as a punishment. Will HUXLEY help them stop the Rogue NPC, or is it planning its own killing rampage to try to escape into the world?

Find out the answers in Rogue NPC, Book 2 of The Bureau of Dangerous Machines series.

About the Author

J. Andrew O'Donnell was born at an early age. He began writing before he could even read, resulting in his early works being complete gibberish. J. began his writing career as a columnist for the Auburn Plainsman at Auburn University in 1995, where he wrote opinion pieces for about four years. He took a brief hiatus from writing to complete his master's degree, get a day job, and raise a family. J. continued his professional writing career after landing a gig as a network security site guide and writer for the New York Times-owned About.com (now known as Lifewire). J's work was selected multiple times to appear on the front page, and he has been featured or mentioned in a variety of publications including NBC News, Scientific American, National Geographic, and Business Insider. The Bureau of Dangerous Machines series was J's first foray into the world of fiction. His latest work: Kill Minus 9, a serialized novel, has received excellent reviews and has held the #1 ranking spot for several of its keywords.

Made in the USA
Columbia, SC
08 October 2022